SOUTH BY SOUTH EAST

Anthony is a popular and prolific children's writer whose books now sell in more than a dozen countries around the world. He has won numerous prizes for his books, which include *Stormbreaker* (shortlisted for the 2000 Children's Book Award) and its sequel *Point Blanc*, about reluctant teenage MI6 spy Alex Rider; *Groosham Grange* and its sequel *The Unholy Grail*; *Granny* (shortlisted for the 1994 Children's Book Award); and the Diamond Brothers trilogy – *The Falcon's Malteser* (which has been filmed with the title *Just Ask for Diamond*), followed by *South by South East* (which was dramatized in six parts on TV) and *Public Enemy Number Two* – to which three short novels have been added: *I Know What You Did Last Wednesday*, *The French Confection* and *The Blurred Man*. Anthony also writes extensively for TV, with credits including the hit series *Murder in Mind*, as well as *Foyle's War*, *Midsomer Murders*, *Poirot* and *Murder Most Horrid*, and he has been described by the *Radio Times* as "a one man crime-wave". He is married to the television producer Jill Green and lives in north London with his two children, Nicholas and Cassian, and their dog, Unlucky.

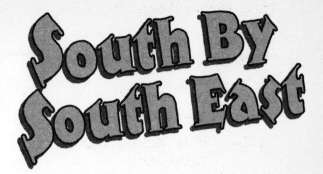

South By South East

ANTHONY HOROWITZ

WALKER BOOKS
AND SUBSIDIARIES
LONDON • BOSTON • SYDNEY

First published 1997 by Walker Books Ltd
87 Vauxhall Walk, London SE11 5HJ

This edition published 2002

4 6 8 10 9 7 5 3

This book has been typeset in Sabon

Printed in Great Britain by Cox & Wyman Ltd, Reading, Berkshire

British Library Cataloguing in Publication Data:
a catalogue record for this book is
available from the British Library

ISBN 0-7445-9037-X

CONTENTS

McGUFFIN

What can I tell you about Camden Town? It's a place in north London with a market and a canal. What you can't find in the market you'll find floating in the canal – only cheaper.

And that's why we'd moved to Camden Town. Because it was cheap. Our new offices were small and sleazy but that was OK because so were most of our clients. We hadn't taken much with us. Just some old furniture and some bad memories. And the door. It was cheaper to bring the door with us than get another one painted.

TIM DIAMOND INC.
PRIVATE DETECTIVE

That's what it said on the glass.

They were the last words Jake McGuffin ever read. But when you're being chased by two Dutch killers with a knife and a gun and your name on both of them, you don't have time to start a paperback book.

It was a long, hot summer. Although I didn't know it then, it was going to be longer and hotter for me than for anyone else. The day it all started, it was my turn to make lunch – but I'd just discovered there was no lunch left to make. I'd done my best. I'd got a tray ready with plates, knives, forks, napkins and even a flower I'd found growing on the bathroom wall. All that was missing was the food.

"Is that it?" Tim asked as I carried it in. He was sitting behind his desk, making paper boats out of pages from the phone book. "A carton of milk?"

"Half a carton," I replied. "We had the other half for breakfast." It was true. Half a carton of long-life milk was all that stood between us and starvation. "I'll get some glasses," I said.

"Don't bother." Tim reached for a cardboard box on the corner of his desk. He turned it upside down. A single straw fell out. "That's the last straw," he announced.

I'd been living with my big brother, Herbert Timothy Simple, ever since my parents decided to emigrate to Australia. Herbert called himself Tim Diamond. He also called himself a private detective. Neither was true. He wouldn't have been able to find a fingerprint on the end of his own finger. Dead bodies made him feel queasy. When it came to pursuing an investigation, he was so hopeless

8

that the investigation usually ended up pursuing him.

I gazed sadly at the milk. "You need a job, Tim," I said.

"I've applied for jobs, Nick," Tim protested. He slid open a drawer in his desk. It was bulging with letters. "Look! I've applied for hundreds of jobs."

"How many rejections have you had?" I asked.

He scowled. "These *are* the rejections." He fumbled in the pile for a minute and pulled one out, his face brightening. "Here's one I haven't heard from yet," he said.

"Maybe your application got lost in the post."

Tim opened the letter and spread it out in front of him. "Head of Security at the Canadian Bank in Pall Mall," he read out. "Forty thousand quid a year plus luncheon vouchers and car. In other words, meals and wheels."

"When will you hear?" I asked.

"Don't worry. The phone'll ring…"

"We don't have a phone," I reminded him. "We got cut off."

Tim's face fell. He folded the letter and put it back in the drawer.

"Things aren't so bad," he muttered. "I'll get a case sooner or later. I bet you any day now somebody's going to knock on the door."

Somebody knocked on the door.

Tim gulped like he'd just swallowed a chicken bone. He looked around him. What with the lunch tray on the desk, the paper boats and everything else, the office hardly looked like the headquarters of a successful private eye. And here was a potential client knocking at the door! For a moment he froze. Then we both went into action.

The paper boats went into the bin. Tim opened another drawer and threw the knives, forks and napkins inside. At the same time, I grabbed the milk carton and slipped it into a vase on a shelf. That just left the tray. Tim handed it to me. I looked for somewhere to put it. I couldn't see anywhere so I put it on a chair and sat on it.

"Come in!" Tim called out. He was bent over the desk, scribbling away at a blank sheet of paper. It would have looked more impressive if he'd been using the right end of the pen.

The door opened.

Our visitor was carrying a gun – and it was the gun that I looked at first. It was small, snubnosed, a dull, metallic grey. So was the visitor. He was only a little taller than me and he was so pale he could have just stepped out of one of those old black and white films they show on TV. He had a square chin, close-cropped hair and small eyes that seemed to be hiding behind the thick lenses of his spectacles. Either he was extremely short-sighted or his optician was. Or maybe it was just that he felt safer behind bulletproof glasses.

He shut the door behind him. It must have been raining outside because there were big drops clinging to his forehead and dripping off the hem of his coat. Or maybe he was sweating. "You Tim Diamond?" he asked.

"Yeah, I'm Tim Diamond," Tim agreed.

The man moved further into the room and saw me. For a moment the gun pointed my way and my hands flickered automatically towards a position somewhere above my head. "Who are you?" he demanded.

"I'm Nick Diamond," I said. "His brother."

His eyes travelled down. "Why are you sitting on a tray?" he demanded.

"Because I feel like a cup of tea." It was the first thing to come into my head but the answer must have satisfied him because a moment later, walking over to the window he'd forgotten me.

"I didn't catch your name," Tim said.

"Jake McGuffin." The man peered out of the window, his eyes as narrow as the venetian blind we'd sold the week before. He glanced back over his shoulder at the door. "Is that the only way in?"

Tim nodded. "Are you in some sort of trouble?" he asked.

"Somebody's trying to kill me," McGuffin said.

He turned away from the window just as a high-velocity bullet fired from the street drilled a neat hole through the pane, flashed across the room a bare millimetre from his face, smashed the vase on the shelf opposite and exposed the carton of milk I had hidden there earlier. Milk fountained out.

"What makes you think that, Mr McStuffing?" Tim enquired.

I was staggered. Even McGuffin had gone pale. But evidently Tim just hadn't noticed there was anything wrong. The truth was he was so wrapped up in his own performance that he probably wouldn't have noticed if his visitor had been hit then and there. I edged closer to the filing cabinet, ready to hurl myself behind it if any more bullets blasted into the room.

McGuffin slipped the gun into a shoulder holster and moved across the carpet, keeping clear of the window. "I need to use a phone," he said. The words came out fast, urgent.

"Why?" Tim asked.

McGuffin hesitated. I think he still hadn't worked Tim out. But then he had other things on his mind.

"You can tell me, Mr McMuffin," Tim went on. He tapped his nose. "I'm a private nose with an eye for trouble. Trouble is my middle name."

McGuffin looked around the room. If he could have seen a telephone I reckon he would have used the flex to strangle Tim and then made his call uninterrupted. But whoever was waiting for him outside had him cornered. Time was running out. He had no choice. "OK," he said. "I'll tell you."

He sat down opposite Tim and took out a cigarette. "You got a light?" he asked.

Tim switched on his desk light. McGuffin scrunched his cigarette on the desktop. He seemed to have got a lot older in the last few minutes. "Listen," he said. "I'm an agent. It doesn't matter who I work for."

"Who *do* you work for?" Tim asked.

"It doesn't matter. I'm on the track of a man called Charon. He's a killer, an assassin, the head of a murder organization that's bigger than Esso."

Tim was puzzled. "Charon?" he asked. "What sort of name is that?"

"It's a code name," McGuffin explained. "It comes out of the Greek myths. You ever hear of Hades, the Greek underworld? In the old legends, it's where people went when they died. Charon was the person who took them there. He was the ferryman of the dead."

The sun must have gone behind a cloud. For the first time that summer I felt cold. Maybe it was the breeze coming in through the bullet hole.

"Nobody knows who Charon really is," McGuffin went on. "He can disguise himself at the drop of a hat. They say he's got so many

13

faces his own mother wouldn't recognize him."

"Do you know his mother?" Tim asked.

"No." McGuffin took a deep breath. "There's only one way to recognize Charon," he said. "He's lost a finger."

"Whose finger?" Tim asked.

"His own. He only has nine fingers."

Tim smiled. "So that'll help you finger him!"

McGuffin closed his eyes for a few seconds. He must have hoped he was dreaming and that when he opened them he'd be somewhere else. "Right," he said at last. "But I've got no time. Charon is about to kill a Russian diplomat called Boris Kusenov."

"I've heard of him," I muttered. And it was true. I'd seen the name in the last newspaper I'd read. It had been underneath my chips.

"If Kusenov dies, that's it," McGuffin went on. "The Iron Curtain goes back up. There'll be another arms race. Maybe even war..."

"As bad as that?" Tim asked.

"I'm the only man who can stop him. I know when Charon plans to kill him. And I know how. I've got to make that call."

Tim shrugged. "That's too bad, McNothing. We don't have a phone."

"No phone..." For a moment I thought he was going to murder Tim. He'd told us everything. And he'd got nothing for it. His hands writhed briefly. Maybe he was imagining them round Tim's throat.

"There's a phone box round the corner, in Skin Lane," I suggested.

McGuffin had forgotten I was even in the room. He looked at me, then at the bullet hole. The bullet hole was like a single eye and that seemed to be looking at me too. "It's an alley," I added.

"Outside." McGuffin licked his lips. I could see his problem. If he waited here much longer, Charon would come in and get him. And next time it might not be a single bullet. One grenade and we'd all be permanently disconnected, like the telephone. On the other hand, if he stepped out into the street he'd be a walking target. And I doubted if Charon would miss a second time.

But McGuffin was obviously used to thinking on his feet. Suddenly he was out of the chair and over the other side of the room where Tim's raincoat was hanging on a hook. "I'll give you fifty pounds for the coat," McGuffin said.

"But you've already got a coat," Tim observed.

"I've got to get out of here without being seen."

McGuffin pulled off his own coat. Underneath he was wearing an off-white suit that had probably been white when he put it on.

It didn't quite hide the gun, jutting out of a shoulder holster where most people carry a wallet. He put on the raincoat, folding the collar up so that it hid most of his face. Finally he produced fifty pounds out of nowhere and threw them down on the desk, five ten pound notes which were the best thing I'd seen all day. Tim wasn't going to complain either. The coat had only cost him ten pounds in the Oxfam shop and even they had probably made enough profit out of it to buy another ox.

McGuffin took a deep breath. He hesitated for one last moment. And then he was gone. The door clicked shut behind him.

I got off the tray. "What do you think?" I asked.

Tim opened his eyes. The money was sitting right in front of him. "Fifty quid!" he exclaimed.

"I wonder who he was working for?"

"Forget it, Nick," Tim pocketed the money. "It's none of our business. I'm just glad we're not involved."

I picked up McGuffin's coat, meaning to hang it back on the hook. As I lifted it, something fell out of one of the pockets. It was a key. There was a plastic tag attached to it and in bright red letters: *Room 605, London International Hotel.*

I looked at the key. Tim looked at me. We were involved all right.

SOUTH BY SOUTH EAST

Maybe I should have emigrated to Australia.

My parents had left the country three years before when I was eleven, and of course they'd meant to take me with them. I'd got as far as Heathrow. But while my parents had got jammed up in one door of the aircraft, I'd slipped out another. Then I'd legged it across the main runway, leaving the screams of the engines – and of my mother – behind me. I remember stopping at the perimeter fence and turning round. And there they were, my mum and dad, flying off to Australia without me. As the plane soared away into the setting sun there was a big lump in my throat and I realized I'd laughed so much I'd swallowed my chewing-gum.

Ever since then I'd been living with Tim. Twice I'd almost been killed with him. I should have remembered that as we set off together in search of McGuffin. Perhaps this was going to be third time unlucky.

"Are you sure about this?" Tim asked as we walked together.

I jiggled the key in my hand. "We're just going to give it back," I said.

As we approached Skin Lane, a street cleaner limped round the corner, stabbing at the pavement with a broken, worn-out brush. The cleaner wasn't looking much better himself. Maybe it was the heat. There was a dustcart parked in the alley and that puzzled me. Why hadn't the cleaner taken the cart with him? Meanwhile Tim had walked on and, looking past him, I saw Jake McGuffin standing in the telephone box with the receiver propped under his chin.

"He's still there," I said.

"Yes." Tim sniffed. "But look at that. He's only had my coat five minutes and he's already spilled something all down the front."

"What?" Suddenly I wasn't feeling so good. The hairs on the back of my neck were standing up, which was strange, because I didn't know I had any hairs on the back of my neck. Leaving the cart, I moved quickly past Tim. McGuffin watched me approach but his eyes didn't focus. I reached out to open the door.

"Wait a minute, Nick," Tim said. "He hasn't finished talking."

I opened the door.

McGuffin had finished talking. The telephone was dead and any minute now he'd be joining it. The stuff he had spilled down the coat was blood, his own blood, and it was Charon who had done the spilling. Even as I opened the door I saw the shattered pane of glass where the bullet had passed through on its way to McGuffin's heart. And at the same time, I knew that the man with the broom – Charon – had just made a clean getaway.

I was holding the door. For a moment I was trapped behind it. Tim was standing in front of me, his mouth open, his eyes wide. Then McGuffin pitched forward, landing in Tim's arms. He was still alive. He began to talk. I would have heard what he said but it was exactly then that a train decided to pass overhead, and for the next few seconds the air was filled with the noise of grinding, creaking metal. The brick walls of the alley caught the sound and batted it back and forth like a ping-pong ball. I saw McGuffin's lips move. I saw Tim nod. But I didn't hear a word. I tried to move round but the glass door was still between me and them. By the time I managed to close it and get over to them, the train was gone.

So was McGuffin.

Tim let him go and he sprawled out on the tarmac. I tried to talk but my lips were too dry. I took a deep breath and tried again. "What did he say?" I asked.

"Suth," Tim said.

"Suth? You mean – south?"

"Yes."

"Was that all?"

"No. He said 'bee'."

"A bumblebee?"

"No." Tim shook his head. "Just 'bee'."

"South. Bee…"

"Suff-iss."

"Suff-iss?"

Tim looked at me sadly. "I couldn't hear," he wailed. "The train was too loud…"

"I know!" I forced myself not to shout at him. "But you were closest to him, Tim. You must have heard what he said."

"I've told you. Suff. Bee. Suff-iss."

"Suff. Bee. Suff-iss?" I played it over in my head a few times. "You mean south by south east? Was that what he said?"

Tim brightened. "Yes! That was it, Nick! I mean, that's what it must have been. South by south east! That's exactly what he said."

"South by south east." I made a quick calculation, then turned round so that I faced the corner of Skin Lane, away from the High Street.

"A dead end," Tim said. He looked down at the body, his face going the colour of mouldy cheese. If we stayed here much longer he was going to pass out on me.

"You're not going to faint, are you?" I asked.

"No!" Tim was indignant.

"You usually faint when there's a dead body."

"No I don't."

"You even fainted when your goldfish died."

"That was grief!"

"We'd better call the police," I said.

Tim glanced at the phone box but I shook my head. "We can't use that one. Finger-prints…"

We half walked, half ran. The police station was a half-mile away. It seemed we were doing everything by halves. It even took us half an hour to get there. The trouble was that Tim was seeing Charon all over the place now. A woman with a pram, a traffic warden, a man waiting for a bus … they all had him paralysed with terror and he would only speak to the desk sergeant in the station when he had counted his ten fingers.

The desk sergeant listened to our story with a cold smile, then showed us into a back room while he went to find a senior officer. I was beginning to wonder if we hadn't made a mistake going there.

Then the door opened and I *knew* we'd made a mistake.

The senior police officer was Chief Inspector Snape.

Snape was a tough, round-shouldered bull of a man. Wave a red flag at him and he'd probably flatten you. He had the sort of flesh you'd expect to see hanging upside down in a butcher's shop. Snape hardly ever smiled. It was as if nobody had taught him how. When his lips did twitch upwards, his eyes stayed small and cold.

But without any doubt, the worst thing about Snape was his sidekick, Boyle. And with Boyle, kick was exactly the word. Boyle loved violence. I once saw a photograph of him in full riot gear – shield, truncheon, tear gas, grenade, helmet – and that had been taken on his day off. He was shorter than Snape, with dark, curly hair that probably went all the way down to his feet.

"Well, well, well," Snape muttered. "If it isn't Tim Diamond!"

"But it is!" Tim replied, brilliantly.

"I know it is!"

Snape's eyes glazed over. Perhaps he was remembering the time when Tim had put together an Identikit picture and the entire police force of Great Britain had spent two months looking for a man with three eyes and an upside-down mouth. "There never was another police constable like you," he rasped.

"Thank you, Chief." Tim grinned.

"I'm not flattering you! I fired you!" Snape had gone bright red. He pulled out a chair and threw himself into it, breathing heavily.

Boyle edged forward. "Are you all right, sir?"

"Yes. I'm all right, Boyle."

"You want me to…" Boyle winked and nodded his head in Tim's direction.

"No. I'm all right." Snape seemed to have collected himself. He glanced at a typed sheet of paper. "So what is all this nonsense?" he demanded. "Spies and killers and bodies in telephone boxes."

"It's the truth," I said.

That brought a dark look from Boyle. "I'll get the truth," he growled.

"No, Boyle." Snape shook his head tiredly.

"I can use the lie detector, sir."

"No, Boyle. You short-circuited it – remember?"

"Look, Chief Inspector," I said. "If you don't believe us, why don't you come back with us? We can show you the body."

Snape considered. "All right," he said. "We'll come with you and take a look. But I warn you, laddie. If you're wasting our time…"

I've been in a police car quite a few times and normally it's fun. But Snape was a slow driver. He didn't put on the siren and the only flashing light was his petrol gauge. By the time we got back to Skin Lane, events had overtaken us. So had half the traffic in London.

He parked the car. We got out. Tim and I had shared the back seat and we were a few paces behind Snape as he turned the corner into the alley. Boyle went between us. We all stopped at the same moment.

"Well?" Snape demanded.

Tim's mouth dropped open. "It's gone," he said.

I looked past him. He was right. McGuffin's body had vanished. But that wasn't the strange part.

So had the telephone box.

ROOM SERVICE

"I don't think Snape believed my story," Tim said.

"Whatever makes you think that, Tim?" I asked.

We'd just been thrown into prison for wasting police time. We were sitting on two bunk beds in a small square cell lit by a single bulb.

Snape hadn't believed a word we'd said – but for once I couldn't blame him. I mean, how often do secret agents drop in on you, swap coats, get shot and then vanish in a puff of smoke, taking the nearest telephone box with them? Even Tim was having trouble working it out.

"Maybe somebody stole the telephone box," he muttered.

"What about the body?" I asked.

"No. It couldn't have been the body, Nick. The body was dead."

Something hard was jabbing into my pocket. At first I thought it was the mattress but as I shifted my weight I realized it was the hotel key. In the excitement I'd forgotten all about it. I suppose I could have shown it to Snape, but I don't think it would have helped. By the time he got to the London International Hotel the whole place would probably have vanished too.

I took the key out and held it up. It took Tim a moment or two to remember what it was. Then he groaned.

"We've got to go there," I said. "Room 605—"

"Why?" Tim cut in.

"You heard what McGuffin said. If this Russian of his gets killed, he was talking about nuclear war … the end of the world!"

"Maybe he was exaggerating."

"Well, *somebody* believed him, Tim."

"How do you know?"

"They shot him."

Snape let us out the next morning with another warning about wasting police time. I noticed that he hadn't wasted a police breakfast on us, and the first thing we did was get a McBreakfast at the nearest McDonald's. We left the place feeling slightly McSick and hopped on a bus that took us across town to the London International Hotel.

The hotel was one of those great piles on twenty-seven storeys with hot and cold running tourists in every room. This was the middle of the summer season, and the building was packed with Japanese and Germans and Scandinavians all milling round searching for someone who could speak their language and knew where Harrods was.

Nobody stopped us as we made our way across to the lift and took it up to the sixth floor, and there was nobody around in the corridor either. We walked on and arrived at room 605. It was a door just like all the others. So why did it seem so solid, so threatening? I handed Tim the key.

"You want me to open it?" he asked.

"Yeah," I said.

"But we don't know what's on the other side."

"That's why we've got to open it."

I knocked on the door first, just to be sure.

Then I stood back while Tim opened it with the key. We slipped in quickly and shut the door behind us. And there we were, inside Jake McGuffin's room. I wondered how long it would be before the hotel realized he'd checked out. Permanently.

There was nobody there. I don't know what I'd been expecting but it was just an ordinary hotel room: twin beds, bathroom and colour TV. It had a nice view of Hyde Park and windows that didn't open so you couldn't throw yourself out when the bill arrived. The beds hadn't been slept in, of course, but there was still some of McGuffin's stuff spread about – a couple of ties on the back of a chair, a pen on the table, a suitcase on the stand by the door.

"There's no one here," Tim said.

"OK. Let's move."

I started with the suitcase but there was nothing interesting inside it, just some shirts and socks and a couple of handkerchiefs. Meanwhile Tim had thrown open the bedside cupboard and was rummaging about inside.

"Nick?" he demanded suddenly.

"Yes?"

"What are we searching for?"

It was a good question, only maybe he should have asked it five minutes before. I shut the suitcase. "We've got to find out who McGuffin was working for and where he'd been," I said. "Anything that can lead us to Charon. Names, addresses, telephone numbers…"

"Sure." Tim snatched up a book of matches lying in an ashtray beside the bed.

"London International," he muttered. "I've heard that name somewhere before."

"Yes, Tim," I said. "It's the name of this hotel."

"Right." He put the matches down and

28

looked underneath the pillows. I didn't know what he hoped to find there. I thought it better not to ask.

In the meantime, I'd crossed over to the low table that ran underneath a mirror along the far wall – and that was where I found it. It was a ticket: seat number 86 to something called the Amstel Ijsbaan. Whatever the something was, it had to be foreign. The only word in the English language that I know with a double "a" in it is "Aagh". The ticket had a little illustration in one corner: a pair of skating boots.

"Come and look at this!" I called Tim over and handed him the ticket.

He examined it. "Do you think he was an ice-skater?" he asked.

"McGuffin?" I shook my head. "He didn't look like one."

"You're right," Tim agreed. "He wasn't wearing shiny tights."

I took the ticket back. "Maybe he was going to meet somebody there," I said.

"Amstel Ix-barn." Tim turned the words over in his mouth. "Do you think it's a play?"

"Not a very catchy title," I muttered.

There was a sudden rattle at the door. Both of us froze. Somebody was trying a key in the lock and somehow I got the feeling it wasn't room service. "Quick!" I whispered. I gestured at the bathroom. As the main door opened we disappeared inside. I took the ticket with me.

Two men came into the bedroom. I had swung the bathroom door shut behind me but left a crack so I could see them. The first man was thin and pale, about thirty-five years old, dressed in a dark suit with hair cut so close that when he spoke you could see the skin move on his skull. The second man was exactly the same. Maybe they hadn't been born twins but whatever work they did had turned them into mirror reflections of each other. They even wore the same sunglasses. You couldn't see their eyes.

"OK, Ed," the first one said. "This is the room."

"Right, Ted."

The second one – Ed – moved forward and grabbed McGuffin's suitcase. Then he started throwing things into it ... the ties, the pen, everything McGuffin had left behind. Meanwhile Ted had pulled a mobile phone out of his jacket pocket and was talking quietly to someone somewhere outside.

"Red? This is Ted. I'm here with Ed. You wait with Ned. We'll be five minutes." He switched it off. "Come on! Let's move it," he muttered. His accent was faintly American but I got the feeling he was English.

"I'll clear the bathroom," Ed announced.

Ed was already moving towards the door. I just had time to grab hold of Tim and jerk him backwards into the bath. As Ed opened the bathroom door, I swept the shower curtain across but it was still a close thing. As he busied himself at the sink, scooping up McGuffin's toothbrush and razor, he was only separated from us by a thin sheet of plastic. Next to me, Tim seemed to be crying. I wondered what had upset him. Then I looked up and realized that the shower was dripping on his nose.

Ed moved out. We got out of the bath and went to the door. Tim had snatched up a lavatory brush in self-defence.

The two men had cleared the room. All McGuffin's things were in his suitcase and the suitcase was in Ted's hand. And that might have been it. They might have walked out of there and been none the wiser. But it had been Tim who had opened the door to McGuffin's room. He had had the key in his hand. And he had left it on the bed. I saw it about half a second before Ted. Then Ted saw it.

"Ed!" he said.

"Ted?"

"The bed!"

Ed looked at the bed and saw the key lying on top of the duvet. As one, the two men's heads turned towards the bathroom. Ted reached into his jacket and pulled out a gun. Then he started moving towards the bathroom. Things looked bad. I was trapped in the bathroom with a quivering brother and a lavatory brush. There was no other way out.

And then, suddenly, the bedroom door opened. Ted spun round. The gun vanished so fast that if he'd missed the holster he'd have stabbed himself with it. A housemaid had chosen that moment to walk into the room. She stood there now with a pile of fresh towels in her hands. She seemed a little surprised to see the two men.

"Excuse me," she said. "I have new towels."

I realized it was time to move. Grabbing a towel off the handrail I walked straight out of the bathroom with Tim close behind. I didn't even look at Ed and Ted. I knew I had to move quickly. The way Ted had concealed the gun told me that he didn't want to start any shooting with witnesses about. Before he had time to change his mind I had walked up to Ed and Ted as if I worked for the hotel too.

"Hi," I said. "These are the old towels."

"Yes," Tim added. "They're very old."

I threw the towels at the two men and ran.

We sprinted out of the room and back down the corridor. I knew that Ed and Ted were close behind us. I'd heard them curse and now their feet were thudding down on the soft-pile carpet. The corridor seemed to stretch on for ever and I couldn't remember the way to the lift. I thought of turning and somehow fighting it out but I knew it was a bad idea. Find people. Instinct told me. You'll be safe in a crowd.

32

Luck must have been on my side because we found the lift just as it reached the sixth floor and the door slid open. I dived in and stabbed at a button. I didn't even notice which one. I just wanted the door to close before Ed and Ted arrived. The door seemed to be taking for ever. Then I realized Tim was leaning on it. I yanked him out of the way. The door slid shut and there was a soft hum as we began to go down. It wasn't the lift that was humming, by the way. It was Tim. I think it must have been the relief.

The lift carried us all the way down to the ground floor and the moment the doors opened we were out. We crossed the lobby and went through the revolving doors. No sooner were we in the sunlight than a taxi drew up in front of us. Even then I thought it was a little odd. There was a taxi rank to one side with several cabs waiting. But this one had come from nowhere, jumping the queue.

"Where to?" the driver asked.

I threw open the door and got in. "Camden Town," Tim said. I looked through the back window. There was no sign of Ed or Ted.

But as we set off, there was a nasty feeling in my stomach and I knew it wasn't car sickness. The driver took a left turn, then a right. Which was funny, because if I'd been going to Camden Town, I'd have taken a right turn, then a left.

"We're going the wrong way," I said.

"What...?" Tim began.

The driver pressed a button and there was a loud click as the cab doors locked themselves automatically. Then he put his foot down on the accelerator and Tim and I were thrown back into our seats as the cab rocketed round a corner.

The driver wasn't going anywhere near Camden Town. We were prisoners on a one-way journey to who-could-say where. Well, one thing was certain. We wouldn't be leaving a tip.

NUMBER SEVENTEEN

The taxi took us into the centre of London, down Oxford Street and into the shabby end of Clerkenwell. We turned into Kelly Street, a road that went from nowhere to nowhere with nothing worth visiting on the way and stopped at Number Seventeen. It was a broken-down red-brick building on four floors. You entered through a set of glass doors. Immediately behind them was a wide empty space that might once have been a shop. Now all it was selling was dust.

"Out!"

The driver was a man of few words, but then "thank you" and "goodbye" would have been enough words for me. Now that I'd taken a closer look at him, I saw that he'd come off the same assembly line that had produced Ed and Ted and I guessed they must have telephoned him from the hotel. He had the same sort of gun too. And he was pointing it at us in just the same way.

He'd unlocked the doors and we got out of the taxi and walked towards the glass doors. There was nobody in sight in Kelly Street. Otherwise we might have tried to make a break for it. I hesitated, but only for a moment.

"Kidnap *and* murder," I said. "You think you can get away with it?"

"Yeah," Tim added. He nodded at the cab. "And you've parked on a yellow line."

"Just keep moving," the driver said, waving.

He led us down a corridor and through a door that opened on to a bare, uncarpeted staircase. The concrete felt cold underneath my feet as we climbed up and I wondered who or what would be waiting for us at the top. There was a rusting fire extinguisher attached to the wall. The driver reached out and turned the tap. It looked as if he'd gone crazy. There was no fire that I could see and anyway no water was coming out. A moment later I understood. Part of the wall swung open – a secret door, and the extinguisher was the handle.

"That's very neat," I said. "But what do you do if the place catches fire?"

We stepped through the wall. And suddenly we were surrounded.

There were people everywhere. In front of the entrance there was a pretty receptionist taking calls on an even prettier telephone system. I hadn't seen so many flashing lights since Christmas. There were five or six offices on either side and the central area was being criss-crossed by suits with men inside. You could hear the jangle of telephones from every direction and voices talking softly like they were frightened of being overheard or even, for that matter, heard.

"Tim...!"

I nudged Tim and pointed. Another door had opened and I could see into what looked like a fully working laboratory with its own collection of technicians in white coats. But you didn't need a microscope to see what they were working on. They had the telephone box from the alley. And they were taking it apart piece by piece. I watched as one man sprayed the glass with some sort of powder while another unscrewed the telephone receiver. But then the taxi driver prodded me with his gun and gestured at the door nearest the receptionist. "In there," he said.

We went in. It was an office like any other with a desk, a computer screen, a few leather chairs and lighting as soft as the executive carpet. Sitting behind the desk was an elderly man with grey hair that had probably come with the job. He was a black man, dressed in a three-piece suit and an old school tie. His movements were slow, but his narrow, grey eyes seemed to move fast.

"Please sit down," he said. "I'll be with you in a minute." He punched a few letters on his keyboard but the screen was turned towards him so I couldn't see what he was writing. Meanwhile, Tim had shifted onto the edge of his seat and was craning to look over the top of the desk. The man noticed him and stopped typing. "Is there something wrong?" he enquired.

Tim coughed. "You're only using two fingers," he said.

"Yes." The man smiled and held up his hands. "But I do have a complete set." He pushed the keyboard away. "So you know about Charon?"

"Maybe…"

"Of course you do, Mr Diamond. You are Tim Diamond, I presume?"

Tim stared. "How do you know that?"

"I was guessing. We found a name tag in the coat that McGuffin was wearing when he … left the company." I couldn't help smiling at that. "I presume he exchanged coats with you in an attempt to escape from Charon. That was the sort of thing McGuffin would have tried. And you must have found the hotel key in his coat. Am I correct?"

"Keep talking," Tim muttered.

"I have your details here on the computer," the old man went on. He glanced at the

38

screen. "Tim Diamond Inc. Detective Agency. Camden Town." He turned to me. "You're not on my file."

"I'm his brother," I said.

"Ah." He typed a few words onto the screen.

"Nick Diamond. Want me to spell it?"

"I think I can manage."

"And what exactly is it that you do manage, Mr..." Tim began.

"My name is Mr Waverly." He smiled. "I am the chief executive of this organization."

"And what organization is that?"

Waverly lowered his voice. "I take it you've heard of MI6."

"I've driven up it," Tim said.

"No," Waverly corrected him. "You're thinking of the M6 motorway to Birmingham. I'm talking about intelligence."

Tim's face brightened. "Then you're talking to the right person!" he announced.

"Military intelligence!" Waverly explained.

"Spies," I added.

"McGuffin was an agent working for me," Waverly went on. "He was pursuing a killer known only as Charon. I don't know how much he had told you, but Charon has a contract on a Russian diplomat by the name of Boris Kusenov."

"How do you know that?" I asked. I didn't

39

think it was an important question when I asked it. It was just something I wanted to know. But it seemed I'd touched on a sore point because suddenly he looked less like the head of the British Secret Service and more like a used car salesman with a second-hand secret.

"It doesn't matter how," he said and I realized that it did matter a lot. "All that matters is that he doesn't kill Kusenov on British soil."

"Suppose he stays on the pavement?" Tim asked.

Mr Waverly swallowed hard. "I mean, we have to ensure that Kusenov is not killed while he is anywhere in Britain," he explained, choosing his words carefully. "It would have huge international repercussions. That is why it is essential that you tell me everything McGuffin told you."

"But he didn't tell us anything," I said.

"That's right," Tim agreed. "He wanted to use a telephone but we haven't got one. So he went out to use the one in the alley." He jerked a thumb in the direction of the laboratory. "He was lucky you hadn't taken it before he got there."

"We took the call box *after* he was killed, Mr Diamond," Waverly said. "McGuffin got through to this office. He told us where he was. Then he was shot. So we took the telephone box to search it for clues."

"Did you find any?" I asked.

"Not yet. But he must have left something. McGuffin was a resourceful operative. He was secretive. A loner. But he'll have done everything he can to get a message to us."

There was a pause.

Tim and I glanced at each other. Waverly may have been hiding something, but we had to tell him everything we knew. After all, he was the head of MI6. And that meant he was on our side.

"How about 'south by south east'?" I said.

"What?"

"They were his last words," Tim explained.

"Just that? South by south east?" Waverly tapped the words into the computer then pressed the button that would send them hurtling into the data bank. The screen bleeped a few times. He pressed another button. "Nothing," he muttered.

Tim got to his feet. "Well, there's nothing more we can do for you…" he began.

"Please sit down, Mr Diamond!"

There was a silence of about thirty seconds as he sat there, calculating. He had plans for us. I could see them forming – faster than the computer signals – in those soft, grey eyes. At last he stretched out a hand and pressed a button on his intercom.

"Miss Jones," he said. "Could you get a drink for our guests?" Then he turned back to us. "I have a proposition for you," he said.

"I want you to work for me. We have to find Charon and you can help."

"Now wait a minute…" Tim began.

Waverly ignored him. "We're running out of time, Mr Diamond. Boris Kusenov arrives in England in just a few days' time. But we no longer have any leads. We have no connection with Charon." He took a deep breath. "Except you."

"Me?" Tim squeaked.

"Charon knows that McGuffin spoke to you before he died. When he discovers that you're working for MI6, maybe he'll get worried."

"How will he discover that?" I asked.

"We'll make sure he finds out."

I couldn't believe it. I played back the sentence in my head and realized that was just what it was. A death sentence. We were going to be the bait in a trap for Charon. And if we got wiped out along the way, I don't think Waverly would even send flowers to the funeral.

Even Tim seemed to have come to the same conclusion. "You can't do it!" he exclaimed. "I'm not a secret agent…"

"You are now," Waverly replied.

The door opened and Miss Jones came in, carrying a tray. She was a short, dumpy woman with hair tied up in a bun – but I hardly noticed her. She had two glasses on the tray. They were filled with a green liquid that was almost luminous. Somehow I didn't think it was apple juice.

"I thought you might be thirsty," Waverly said.

"I was until she came in," I replied.

"Please drink..."

It was a command, not an invitation, and I got the feeling that something nasty would happen to us if we refused. Mind you, I knew something nasty was going to happen to us anyway. We didn't have much choice. I held up the glass.

"Down the hatch," Tim said.

"Yeah. And into the coal cellar," I added.

We drank.

The juice tasted sweet and minty – like mouthwash. I think I began to feel its effects even before it had reached my throat.

"I can give you one piece of guidance in your task," Waverly went on, but already his voice was in the next room. He seemed to be shrinking behind the desk, like we were looking at him through the wrong end of a telescope. "McGuffin wasn't working alone. He'd been in touch with the Dutch Secret Service..."

"I didn't know the Dutch had a secret service," I said. The words came out thick and heavy.

"That's how secret they are," Mr Waverly explained. "We don't even know the name of the agent he was working with. But he had a number. 86. Can you remember that?"

"68," Tim said.

"89," I corrected him.

"86," Mr Waverly corrected me.

The room was spinning round and round. Now I knew what a CD felt like. Only instead of music, all I could hear was Waverly's voice, the words slurring together, echoing around me. "You're on your own, Diamond," he was saying. "On your own ... on your own."

"Where's Nick?" Tim asked.

"On the floor," I replied.

A moment later the carpet rushed up at me, and I was.

BIRDS

"Waverly was hiding something," I said.

Tim and I were sitting back in the Camden Town office, which was where we'd woken up. Whatever it was in the drink we had been given, it was powerful stuff. My head was still hurting. My tongue felt like someone had used it to dry the dishes.

"What was he hiding?" Tim asked. He wasn't looking much better than me. It was four o'clock in the afternoon. We'd been unconscious for about six hours.

"I don't know. It was something to do with Boris Kusenov. How did Mr Waverly find out that Charon was planning to kill him? And why is it so important that it doesn't happen in Britain?"

"Maybe it would be bad for the tourist trade."

Tim poured himself a cup of tea. "He

offered me a job!" he exclaimed. "A spy! Working for MI6!"

I shook my head. I didn't want to disillusion him but he had to know. "You're not a spy, Tim," I told him. "You're a sitting target."

Tim stood up. "What do you mean?"

"I mean – when Charon hears you're working for MI6, he'll come gunning for you. Or knifing. Or harpooning. That's what Mr Waverly wants."

"Why? Didn't he like me?"

"If Charon comes after you, he'll be too busy to go after Kusenov. And of course, it gives Waverly another chance to catch him."

"You mean – he's using me?"

"Yes."

"Over my dead body!"

"Exactly..."

Tim sat down again behind his desk. Then he stood up. Then he sat down again. I was beginning to get a crick in my neck watching him, but at last he swung round and I realized that he was actually furious. "How dare he!" he squeaked. "Well, I'm going to show him!"

"What are you going to do?"

"He kidnapped me. He drugged me. And now he's trying to get me killed. What do you think I'm going to do? I'm going to the police!"

"Snape?" I grimaced. "Are you sure that's such a good idea?"

But Tim wouldn't let me talk him out of it. And that was how – the very same day that we'd been released from jail for wasting police time – we found ourselves knocking on the door, asking to be let back in again. The desk sergeant wasn't pleased to see us. We left him chewing the desk while a constable went to fetch Chief Inspector Snape.

Then Snape himself arrived, with Boyle, as ever, just a few steps behind. "I do not believe it!" he exclaimed in a cracked voice.

"But Chief ... I haven't told you yet," Tim replied.

So Tim told him: the hotel room, the two MI6 agents, the taxi ride, Kelly Street, Mr Waverly ... everything. Snape listened without interrupting, but I got the idea that he wasn't taking Tim seriously. Maybe it was the way he rapped his fingernails on the table and stared out of the window. Maybe it was his occasional sniff of silent laughter. Meanwhile Boyle stood with his back against the wall, smirking quietly to himself.

"So that's it?" Snape enquired when Tim had finished. "You really expect me to swallow that?"

"But it's the truth!" Tim insisted. He turned to me. "Tell him!" he exclaimed.

"It's the truth," I agreed. What else could I say?

Snape considered. "Very well," he muttered

at length. "Let's take a look at Number Seventeen. But I'm warning you, Diamond…"

He drove us back to Kelly Street and stopped at the bottom. We walked the last fifty metres – with Snape's driving that had to be the fastest part of the journey. Eleven, thirteen, fifteen … I counted off the numbers of the buildings as we went past. It was all just like I remembered it. Then we reached Number Seventeen.

It wasn't there any more.

At least, there was something there only it wasn't what had been there the last time we were there. It was as confusing as that. The empty window, the dust and the bare floorboards had been replaced by a pretty shop that looked as if it had been there for years. There was a wooden sign above the door that read: *Bodega Birds*. But these weren't the oven-ready variety. You could hear them squawking even out in the street: budgies and canaries and just about every other species of feathered friend. "Hello!" someone shouted. I think it was a parrot.

Tim had seen all this too. "Wait a minute!" he cried in a high-pitched voice. For a moment he sounded remarkably like a parrot himself. "The birds. They weren't there!"

"So how did they get here then?" Snape asked. "I suppose they just flew in?"

"I don't know!"

We went in. I looked for the door that led to the staircase. At least that was still in place, only now you had to step past a row of canaries to reach it. But then there were birds everywhere, twittering in their cages or rocking backwards and forwards on their perches. The back of the shop was lined with shelves stacked high with bird-food, bird-toys, bird-baths and everything else you might need if you happened to be a bird. And none of it was new. As far as we could tell, it had all been there for years.

"This is the wrong place!" Tim said.

"It's Number Seventeen," Snape growled.

"Can I help you?" The speaker was an elderly woman in a bright pink cardigan, white blouse and beads. She had small, black eyes and a pointed nose like a beak. Give her a few feathers and you'd have had difficulty finding her among the birds. She had shuffled round from behind the counter and, with fingers that were thin and bent, began to stroke a big blue parrot.

"Are you the manager here?" Snape asked.

"Yes. I'm Mrs Bodega." Her voice was thin and high-pitched.

"How long has this shop been here?"

Mrs Bodega worked it out on her fingers. "Let me see," she trilled. "I opened the shop two years before my husband died – and that was nine years ago. My husband was pecked to death, you know. The birds did love him! But they didn't know when to stop. So … eight years plus two years. That's ten years in all."

She tickled one of the parrots. The parrot swayed on its perch and preened itself against her. "This is Hercule," she went on. "He was my husband's favourite. We called him Hercule after that nice detective, Hercule Parrot."

At least that amused Boyle. "Hercule Parrot," he muttered and stuck out a finger. The parrot squawked and bit it.

"Are you looking for anything in particular?" Mrs Bodega asked.

Snape turned to Tim. "Well?"

"She's lying!" Tim exclaimed. "This shop wasn't here." He nudged me. "Tell him!"

I had a feeling I was wasting my time but I tried anyway. "It's true," I said. "This is all a fake. And this woman…" I pointed at Mrs Bodega. "She must be some sort of actress."

"I'm no such thing. Who are you? What do you want?"

Boyle pulled his swollen finger out of his mouth and went over to Snape. "Give me five minutes, sir," he pleaded. "Just five minutes. Alone with them."

"No, Boyle," Snape sighed.

"Five minutes with the parrot?"

"No." Snape closed his eyes.

Tim was utterly confused. Mrs Bodega was watching us with a mixture of innocence and

50

indignation. "All right," Snape said. "Just tell me where these agents of yours took you."

"They took us upstairs," Tim said. He pointed. "There's a staircase behind that door."

"There's no such thing!" Mrs Bodega muttered.

"I'll show you!"

Tim marched forward and threw open the door. He'd taken two more steps before he realized what I'd seen at once. The staircase was no longer there. He'd walked into a broom cupboard. There was a crash as he collided with an assortment of buckets and brooms. A shelf gave way and clattered down bringing with it about five years' supply of bird-seed. Tim simply disappeared in a gold-and-white shower of the stuff. It poured down on him, forcing him to his knees, burying him.

And then it was all over. There was a small mountain of bird seed on the floor with two legs jutting out of it. The mountain shifted and broke open. Tim stuck his head out and coughed. Bird seed trickled out of his ear.

Snape had seen enough. "So they took you into a broom cupboard, did they?" he snarled. He caught one of the brooms. "I suppose this was your brush with MI6?"

"Chief Inspector! Listen..."

It was too late for that. Snape dropped the broom and grabbed hold of Tim, and, at the same time, I winced as Boyle's hand clamped itself onto my shoulder. A moment later my feet had left the floor. All around me, the birds were screeching and whistling and fluttering. It was as if they were laughing at us. But then maybe they knew. They weren't the only ones who were going to be spending the night behind bars.

HIGH SECURITY

This time Snape locked us up for two days. Boyle wanted to throw the book at us but fortunately he didn't have a book. I'm not even sure Boyle knew how to read.

As soon as we were released, we headed back to the office. Tim wasn't talking very much. He didn't say anything on the bus, not even when I took the window seat. And he only muttered a few words of surprise when he found a letter waiting for him on our doormat. Not many people ever wrote to Tim. There were the electricity and the gas bills, of course, but they weren't exactly chatty. Mum and Dad sometimes dropped us cards: Australia's hot, England's not, we love you a lot ... that sort of thing. But usually the only letters on the doormat read: *Please wipe your feet*.

This letter came in a smart white envelope, postmarked London. Tim finally opened it in the office while I poured the tea. To celebrate our release, I'd used new teabags. It was a short letter but he took a long time to read it. Maybe it was good news.

"So what is it?" I asked at last.

"It's a job." Tim smiled for the first time since we'd been locked up and passed the letter across to me. It came from the Canadian Bank in Pall Mall and was signed by a woman called Louise Meyer. Briefly, it invited Tim to an interview to discuss the position of Head of Security.

"What is this…?" I began.

"Don't you remember?" Tim said. "I told you. I applied for the job a couple of months ago." He snatched the letter back. "They need a new Head of Security."

"But you don't know anything about security," I said.

"Yes I do!" Tim looked at me indignantly. "I put burglar alarms in the office," he reminded me.

"And burglars stole them," I reminded him. Tim ignored me.

"Aren't you forgetting something?" I went on. "What about Charon? What about MI6?"

"What about them?"

"You can't just ignore them! You heard what McGuffin said. And you still don't know what south by south east means…"

"I don't think it means anything." Tim

sniffed. "Anyway, it's none of my business. Banking is my business."

I gave up. "When's the interview?" I asked.

Tim quickly re-read the letter. "This Meyer woman wants to see me at two o'clock this afternoon," he said. He sprang out of his chair. "This afternoon! That's today!"

It was already half past twelve. The next twenty minutes were spent in a frantic attempt to prepare himself. He put on a suit, a tie and a shirt while I polished his shoes. I didn't do a great job but then I was using furniture polish. Finally he dragged a leather attaché case out of a cupboard. Actually, it wasn't leather – it was kangaroo skin; an unwanted Christmas present. Mum had given it to Tim. Tim had given it to me. I'd given it to Oxfam. They'd given it back. You can't get much more unwanted than that. But now he took it because he thought it made him look good. The clock struck one. He was ready.

"I'll come with you," I said.

"Sure." Tim nodded. "You can wait outside."

We got another bus back into town and this time Tim was in a better mood. He was rehearsing his answers all the way there, whispering to himself and nodding. The other passengers must have thought he was mad. I wasn't even sure myself. But he'd completely forgotten about McGuffin and Charon. That much was obvious. And that was his big mistake.

It happened just as we got off at Pall Mall. There had been about a dozen people on the top deck with us and I hadn't really noticed any of them. But one of them had followed us down and just as we stepped off the bus, he reached out and tapped Tim on the shoulder.

"Excuse me," he said. "You've forgotten this." And he gave Tim back his kangaroo-skin attaché case. That was all there was to it. I got a flash of a dark face and a beard. Then the bus had moved off and we were standing on the pavement. That was all there was to it. But I was uneasy. I didn't know why.

"Tim..." I called out.

But Tim had already arrived outside the Canadian bank. I could tell it was Canadian because of the flag on the roof and the bronze moose on the door. It was a small, square building, one floor only. In fact it looked more like a high-class jeweller's than a High Street bank. Everything about it was quiet and discreet. Even the alarms were muffled so they wouldn't disturb the neighbours. I caught up with Tim just before he went in.

"I think we ought to talk," I said.

"I know what to say," he replied "You wait here."

He went in. I looked at the clock above the door. There wasn't one. And that was strange because when I'd been standing next to Tim, I'd definitely heard the sound of ticking. I thought about the attaché case again. And suddenly the skin on my neck was prickling and my mouth had gone dry. Either Tim was in serious trouble or I was going down with the flu.

It wasn't the flu. I'd never felt better in my life. And now I had to act quickly. I'd hardly glimpsed the man on the bus but I knew now why he had taken the case and what he had put inside it.

I also knew that if I'd stopped to count his fingers, I wouldn't have reached ten.

Tim had disappeared into the bank. I plunged in after him, off the street and into the white marble banking hall. It was cool inside, out of the summer heat. The marble was like ice and even the potted plants seemed to be shivering in the air-conditioning. My eyes swept past the cashiers, the plush leather furniture, the tinkling chandeliers. I saw Tim just as he walked through a door at the far left corner. That had to be Mrs Meyer's office. Gritting my teeth, I prepared to follow him. Somehow I had to get him out of there. Already it might be too late.

I'd taken just one step before a hand clamped down on my shoulder and I was twisted round to face the biggest security guard I'd ever seen.

"What do you want then?" he demanded.

"I want to open an account," I said. It was the first thing to come into my head. He smiled mirthlessly. "Oh yes? I suppose you think this is some sort of piggy-bank?"

"Well they certainly seem to employ a few piggies."

Five seconds later I found myself back out on the street with a neck that felt as though it had been through a mangle. I wondered if the Canadian security guard had ever worked as a lumberjack. He would have only had to smile at a tree to knock it down.

Maybe it was the sun, but the sweat was beginning to trickle down my neck as I walked round behind the bank. It was on a corner, separated from the pavement by a narrow line of flower-beds. Slowly, I tiptoed through the tulips peering in through the ground floor windows. Fortunately, they were fairly low down and because of the hot weather some of them were partly open. I heard snippets of conversation, the jangle of coins, telephones ringing. At the sixth window I heard Tim's voice. He was already being interviewed by Louise Meyer.

"Tell me, Mr Diamond," the manager asked. "Do you have any experience of security?"

"Not exactly security, Lucy," Tim replied. He paused. "Do you mind if I call you Lucy?"

"I prefer to be more formal."

"That's OK, Lucy. You can call me Mr Diamond."

Another tulip snapped underneath my feet as I shifted closer to the window. I reached up to the window-sill, then pulled myself up and looked through the glass.

I could see Tim sitting right in front of me, facing the window. Louise Meyer was opposite him, behind her desk. She was a tough, no-nonsense businesswoman. She was wearing a dark blue suit cut so sharply she could have opened a letter with her sleeve.

"I don't have much experience of security, Lucy," Tim went on. "But I do have the security of experience."

I looked round the office. It was a big room, dominated by the desk, with a few chairs, a cocktail cabinet, a map of Canada and a heavy filing cabinet. There was a sort of alcove just outside the office, a miniature reception area, and I could make out an old-fashioned iron safe jutting out from the wall. Tim had forgotten to bring his case into the office. He had left it on top of the safe.

"So you've never worked in a bank," Louise Meyer said.

"You could say that," Tim replied.

"Well – have you?"

"No."

I waved. Tim was staring right at me but he

59

was so wrapped up in himself that he didn't notice anything. I thought of tapping on the glass but I didn't want Meyer to hear. I just wanted Tim out of there and the attaché case with him.

"But let's talk about your bank, Lou," Tim went on. "Frankly, I'd feel safer leaving my money in a paper bag at a public swimming pool."

"You would?" Mrs Meyer was astonished.

"You've got more holes here than a fishing net. If you ask me, a robber could crack this place in about fifteen seconds flat."

"You think so?"

"I know it." Tim slumped into his chair. He was obviously enjoying himself.

I waved harder, jumped up and down and whistled. Tim ignored me. "Have you checked who I am, Lulu?" he asked the manager. "I could be a crook myself."

"Well…" I saw Mrs Meyer's hand reaching out for the alarm button under her desk.

"I could have a gun on me right now."

"Wait a minute, Mr Diamond." Mrs Meyer was getting nervous and anyone except Tim would have seen it.

"I could have a partner waiting outside…"

"Could you?" Louise Meyer turned in her seat to look out of the window. That was when she saw me. I was frozen with one hand in the air like I was about to punch my way through the glass. I opened my mouth to explain.

"And I could have a bomb," Tim added.

And that, of course, was when the bomb went off.

I didn't even realize what had happened at first. There was a flash of red light and the window seemed to curve out towards me. I must have been off-balance from the start because my legs jackknifed under me and I was thrown back onto the flower-bed. This was just as well. A torrent of burning air and jagged glass missed my head by a fraction as half the office was blown out into the street.

Somehow I managed to get back to my feet. I was glad they were still at the end of my legs. I gave myself a quick examination. There was blood on my shirt and it looked like my colour but otherwise I seemed to be in one piece. It was raining. I blinked. The rain was made of paper. I looked closer and realized what was happening. It was raining money, Canadian dollars and English pounds blown out of the manager's personal safe. As I staggered round to the front door, I snatched a few notes and put them in my pocket. I had a feeling I was going to need them.

Inside, the calm of the bank had been shattered. So had the marble floor. The cashiers were in hysterics, the alarm-bells jangling, the air thick with dust. I couldn't see the security guard, which was probably just as well.

Then I saw Tim. He had walked back into the main banking hall as if he were in a daze, which, in fact, he probably was. His clothes were in rags, his face was black, and he seemed half-stunned. But like me, he was still in one piece.

Then the security guard staggered towards him. At the same time Louise Meyer appeared in the shattered doorway. Her two-piece suit was now a four-piece suit. Her make-up had been blown off. And she was completely covered in dust. Now, with the security guard only millimetres away from Tim, she shouted out, "Don't go near him! He's got a gun!"

"No I haven't," Tim protested.

Suddenly I knew there was only one way out of this. "Yes you have!" I shouted.

"Have I?" Tim saw me. And he understood. "Yes I have!" he exclaimed. "I've got a gun!"

It worked. The cashiers began screaming again and the security guard backed away. For a moment the way out was clear but already I could hear the first police sirens slicing their way through the London traffic. It was time to go.

"Tim!" I shouted. He saw me and ambled over to the door. "Let's get out of here!"

We went. Nobody tried to stop us. As far as they were concerned, we were dangerous criminals. I didn't know where we were going or what we were going to do. I was just glad to be out of there. But as we passed through the front door, Tim stopped and turned round.

"Wait a minute, Nick," he said. "I still haven't heard if I've got the job."

A police car turned the corner. I grabbed Tim and ran.

CHAIN REACTION

One hour after the bank blast, Tim was a wanted man. Suddenly his picture was in the papers and on TV. Identikit pictures had appeared so fast you'd think the police had had them printed in advance just in case they needed them. Once again we were Public Enemies – but all we'd managed to take from the bank was two hundred dollars and some travellers' cheques. I changed the dollars and used some of the money to buy Tim a new shirt. That hardly left enough to get us a room for the night.

We couldn't go back to the office. That was the first place they'd come looking for us. We needed a cheap hotel somewhere quiet, where they didn't look at their guests too closely. Somewhere that needed guests so badly they wouldn't look at all.

We found the hotel on the wrong side of

Paddington. In fact it wasn't a hotel but a guest house; a narrow, grimy building with no name on the door, but a "Vacancies" sign in the window. It was halfway down a cul-de-sac so there would be no passing traffic. And you couldn't reach it from the back either. The Paddington railway tracks cut right through the garden. Try mowing the lawn and you'd be run over by a train.

"What do you think?" Tim asked.

"It's fine," I said. I rang the bell.

The door was opened by a thin, elderly woman in a grey cardigan that she had knitted herself. About halfway through she must have lost the pattern. Underneath it there was a shabby dress hanging over a hideous pair of slippers with pink pom-poms.

"Yes?" she said.

"You got a room?" Tim asked.

"Oh yes! Come in! I've got lots of rooms."

The lady led us through a dark, depressing hallway and into a reception room that wasn't much better.

This room had six lumpy chairs and a coffee-table stained with coffee. Two elderly men were sitting at a table playing chess. A third man was in an armchair with his back to us.

"My name is Mrs Jackson," the lady told us. She spoke like a Duchess, rolling each word between her lips. "Let me introduce you to my guests." She gestured at the plump, fair-haired

65

man in the armchair. "Mr Blondini is in the theatre!" she announced. The man in the arm-chair grinned and tried to stand up. But he couldn't, as he was wearing a straitjacket and there were about a dozen chains snaking round his arms, legs and chest. "Mr Blondini is an escapologist," Mrs Jackson explained.

"Just practising!" Mr Blondini added, heaving frantically with his shoulders.

Mrs Jackson went over to the two men playing chess. The first of them was short with close-cropped hair and a monocle. "This is Mr Webber," she said. "Mr Webber is from Germany. But otherwise he's perfectly nice."

"Check!" Mr Webber snapped, moving his bishop with such force that it snapped too.

"And this is Mr Ferguson." The other player was tall and thin, a timid-looking man with curly hair. Mrs Jackson drew Tim aside. "Do try not to mention mountains or tall buildings to him," she whispered. "Mr Ferguson suffers terribly from vertigo."

Tim waved at Mr Ferguson. "Hi!" he said.

Mr Ferguson rolled his eyes and fainted.

Mrs Jackson frowned. "I have a room on the first floor," she said. "How many nights will it be?"

"We'll be here until the end of the week," I lied.

"It's thirty pounds a night. Cash in advance."

I nodded and Tim counted out three ten pound notes.

Mrs Jackson snatched them hungrily. "Room twelve on the first floor at the end of the corridor," she said. She stopped and looked more closely at Tim. "Do I know you?" she said. "Your face is very familiar. What did you say your name was?"

"It's … it's…" Tim stared blankly at me.

I glanced at the ten pound notes in Mrs Jackson's hands. "It's Queen," I said. "We're the Queen brothers."

"Oh yes?"

"Good night, Mrs Jackson."

I grabbed Tim and we made our way upstairs. At the top, I turned and looked back. The landlady was still there, watching us, her eyes glinting in the half-light. I nodded at her and she spun on her heel, disappearing the way she had come.

"She knows who we are!"

"No, Tim. Maybe she saw you on the news. But I don't think she recognized you…"

We were sitting in room twelve a few minutes later. The room was about as inspiring as the rest of the hotel. It had one ancient bed, a couch and a swirly carpet that had lost most of its swirls. Tim was lying on the bed. I was sitting next to him, thinking. We couldn't stay long at this guest house. Not at thirty pounds a night. We had to go somewhere. But where?

It seemed to me we had only one choice. Tim was now a wanted bank robber. Snape would never believe our story about the bomb, not after the telephone box and the pet shop. No, Mr Waverly – the real Mr Waverly – had us right where he wanted us. We had to help him find Charon. It was our only chance.

But where could we start? Sitting on the bed, I thought about what he had told us. One of his agents, Jake McGuffin, had been following Charon's trail but he hadn't been working alone. Waverly had mentioned a Dutch secret agent. A man with no name – but a number. Seventy-six or eighty-six...

Eighty-six! It meant something to me. I was sure of it. I had seen or heard the number somewhere before. And sitting there on the lumpy mattress, I suddenly remembered where.

"Tim!" I exclaimed. I stood up and pulled the ticket out of my pocket. This was the ticket to the ice-rink that I had found in McGuffin's hotel room. And I was right! There was a number printed in the left-hand corner.

The number was eighty-six.

I showed it to Tim. "Don't you see?" I said. "I think this is a ticket to an ice-rink in Amsterdam. McGuffin and the Dutch agent must use it as a meeting place." I pointed at the two words at the top of the ticket. "Amstel Ijsbaan.

Do you think that sounds Dutch?"

"It's all Greek to me," Tim said.

"Amstel…" Just for once I wished I'd concentrated more in geography lessons. "Isn't that a river," I said. "In Amsterdam?" It was all beginning to make sense. "We have to go there."

"To Amsterdam?"

"We'll find the ice-rink. We'll find 86. And he'll help us find Charon."

"And then what?"

"I don't know, Tim. I'm completely in the dark…"

That was when the lights went out.

Suddenly it was pitch black in the room. At the same time there was a click and a rush of cool air as the door was opened and even as I stood up to take my bearings, I felt myself grabbed and thrown back on the bed. I heard Tim cry out. Then someone grabbed my hand and I felt a circle of cold metal closing around my wrist. There was a second click, closer this time and more distinct. I tried to move my hand and found that I couldn't.

And then the lights went back on and I found myself staring at Mrs Jackson and two of her lodgers – Mr Webber and Mr Ferguson. But that wasn't the worst of it. Tim was lying next to me and now I saw that they had managed to handcuff us together. And, most bizarre of all, Mrs Jackson was holding a gun.

A moment later, Mr Blondini came into the room. He had obviously been the one controlling the main fuse. "Did you get them?" he asked.

"Oh yes!" Mrs Jackson pursed her lips. "Who'd have thought it?" she went on. "A dangerous criminal sleeping in my house!"

"It's not true!" I said.

"That's right!" Tim agreed. "I hadn't gone to bed yet."

"He's not a dangerous criminal!" I explained. "He hasn't done anything!"

"Then why is his face here?" Mr Ferguson asked. He produced a copy of that day's *Evening Standard* with Tim's face on the front page. So that was how they had recognized us.

"We'd better call the police." Mrs Jackson was still aiming the gun at us. She turned to Mr Webber. "Do you know the number?"

"Nine, nine, nine," the German said.

"All right," she muttered. "I'll look it up in the phone book."

"I've already called them," Mr Blondini said. "They're on the way."

"Good!"

I looked around me, trying to find some way out of this situation, but there was nothing I could do, not while Mrs Jackson had the gun. The gun ... I'd been held up at gunpoint quite a few times in my life. The Fat Man, Johnny Powers, Big Ed – they'd all tried it at one time or another. But now I looked at her, I saw there was something wrong about Mrs Jackson. It wasn't just her. It was the way she was holding the gun. Or perhaps it was the gun itself…

And suddenly I knew. "Have you got a cigarette, Mrs Jackson?" I asked.

"You're too young to smoke," she scowled.

"Then why are you offering me a light?" I pointed at the gun. My hand was chained to Tim's and he pointed at it too.

"What…?" Tim began.

The front doorbell rang. The police had arrived.

"Move!" I shouted.

We leapt off the bed and pushed past Mrs Jackson and her friends, making for the door. They were too surprised to do anything and a moment later we were out of the room. I could feel the chain straining at my wrist as Tim hesitated. I suppose he was afraid that we were about to get shot. But I knew better. It hadn't been a real gun at all but a fancy cigarette-lighter. And how had I guessed? Maybe it was just intuition. But the single word "Dunhill" printed on the barrel had probably helped.

Down below, the police were hammering at the door. That meant we could only go up. We found a second staircase and clambered up it, arriving on the second floor. This was also the top floor. We had nowhere else to go. Behind me I heard Mrs Jackson hurrying down to let the police in. We had maybe ten seconds before we were taken.

There was a window at the end of the corridor. Pulling Tim with me, I went over to it. The window was at the back of the house. There was a narrow alley – about two metres across – and then a lower building. The roof of the other building was a few metres below us. It was flat, covered in black asphalt.

"We can jump," I said.

"We can't," Tim quavered.

"We've got to." I opened the window and Tim and I crawled out onto the sill. The handcuffs didn't make it easy. We hovered there for a few seconds. Behind us, I could hear the police racing up the stairs.

"Jump!"

I launched myself into space. Tim did the same. Like some sort of clumsy, prehistoric bird we soared out of the house. For a horrible moment I thought I wasn't going to make it. And if I didn't make it, nor would Tim. The chain would drag him back and we'd both end up as so many broken bones on the pavement below. But then the asphalt roof rushed up and hit me in the chest. My legs still hung in space but enough of me had reached the building to save me. I twisted to the right. Tim was lying beside me.

"Close…" he rasped and wiped his brow. He used the chained hand and I had to wipe

72

his brow too.

The building was some sort of office block. We found a skylight in, a flight of stairs down and a glass door out. Nobody saw us go. There were about a dozen police cars parked in the street at the front but everybody was concentrating on Mrs Jackson's guest house so we simply walked away. We held hands until we were round the corner. But then, of course, we were still very much attached.

TRAIN REACTION

Getting across London again wasn't easy – but we had no choice. If we really were heading for Amsterdam, that meant a ferry from Dover. If we wanted to get to Dover we had to start at Victoria. And that meant holding hands through Hyde Park and on through Knightsbridge to the other side of London.

The chances of our reaching Victoria without being seen must have been a thousand to one against, but somehow we managed it. We emerged in front of the main forecourt where the taxis and buses were locked into what had become a frozen mosaic of black and red. All we had to do now was to find the right train.

"Where's the ticket-office?" I muttered the question more to myself than to Tim but unfortunately he heard me.

"I'll ask," he said. He turned to someone standing nearby. "Excuse me," he went on.

"Can you tell me where the ticket-office is?"

"Certainly, sir. It's through the main entrance and on the left."

It was the "sir" that alerted me. I looked round and nearly died on my feet. Tim had just asked a policeman.

Even then we might have slipped away. But Tim had realized what he had done. He went bright red. He squeaked. He hid his head behind his arm. If the policeman hadn't noticed him before, he couldn't help but look twice then. I hurried Tim away. But it was already too late. Looking back over my shoulder, I saw the policeman staring after us. He was talking into his radio at the same time.

We didn't buy a ticket. I knew that the police would soon be after us and that would be the first place they'd look. Our only chance was to get out of Victoria as quickly as possible on a train. I dragged Tim across the main concourse. There was a train to Dover leaving in nine minutes. Would it pull out before the police pulled in? I decided to take a gamble. We took the train.

As we climbed on, Tim stopped me. "Look!"

I followed his eyes. "Network South East!" he explained.

It was true. We were travelling Network South East. The words were written on the side of the carriage. "So what?" I asked.

"We're going south by South East!" Tim said.

I had to admit that he had a point. South by south east. Was that what McGuffin had meant by his final words? "Let's get on," I said.

We walked down the train, looking for the quietest carriage. We were still chained together of course and I was frightened that somebody might notice. But the other passengers were too busy getting out their sandwiches and newspapers. We had just reached First Class when the train jolted and began to move forward. We were on the way.

The second-class carriages had been almost full. First Class was almost empty. But as I began to move forward again, I noticed a young woman, sitting on her own, reading a book. At least, she *had* been reading the book. Now she was staring at us.

She was a few years older than Tim, dressed in a smart shirt and suit with a silk scarf and grey, suede gloves. I thought she might be an actress or maybe the head of a fashion firm. She had long fair hair, a little make-up and soft, suntanned skin. Her eyes were a shade of green that made me think of cats and Egyptian princesses and witchcraft.

She knew who we were. There could be no doubt of it. "Sit down!" she said.

I hesitated. But I could see we had no choice.

I sat down, pulling Tim with me.

"Tim Diamond!" She smiled as she said the words. As far as she knew, Tim was a wanted criminal, a dangerous bank robber. But she was treating the whole thing like a joke.

"Hello!" Tim's voice sounded peculiar.

I glanced at him. He had gone bright red and his lips were wobbling. For a minute I thought he was train sick. Then I realized it was something much, much worse. Tim had fallen in love.

"I'm Tim," he said. "This is another brick."

"I'm sorry?"

"My brother, Nick," he corrected himself.

The woman glanced at our handcuffs. "Is that chain the one you pull in emergencies or do you always travel like that?" she asked. Her voice had an accent. She wasn't English, that was for sure. But what was she? Who was she? And why hadn't she sounded the alarm?

"I can explain…" I began.

"There's no need to." She smiled again and I had to admit it was a pretty smile. "My name is Charlotte Van Dam," she went on. "I'm Dutch and I'm a writer. Crime stories. I'm on my way home from a convention in London."

"How unconventional," Tim gurgled.

"If you know who he is, how come you aren't calling the cops?" I asked.

She leaned forward and put a hand on Tim's knee. Tim squirmed in his seat and blushed.

"I know an innocent man when I see one," she said. "And your brother has got the most lovely big, wide, innocent eyes."

Yeah. They match his lovely big, wide, innocent brain, I thought. But I decided to say nothing. If Charlotte Van Dam was crazy enough to fancy Tim, that might just help us. And right now we needed all the help we could get.

"So tell me, Timothy," she said. "What takes you to Dover?"

"Well ... the train does," Tim replied. As brilliant as ever.

"You're on the run from the police!" she whispered. And now I understood. She'd been writing crime fiction all her life but now she'd just met the real thing. No wonder she was excited. "Are you going to leave the country?" she asked.

In the end we told her the whole story, just as we had told Snape a few days before. The only difference was that she believed us. And not only did she believe us – she was enthralled.

"I want to help!" she gasped, when we had finished. "I can find this man you're seeking."

"86?" I said.

"Yes. The secret agent. I can go to the Amstel Ijsbaan for you. I live in Amsterdam. I speak the language. Please, you must let me go!"

Tim shook his head. "But Charlotte, it could be dangerous."

"Charon could be there," I agreed.

"Yes. And you might slip on the ice," Tim added.

Charlotte moved closer to Tim and looked at him adoringly. I could almost hear the violins playing in the background. She was in love with Tim! It was incredible. "You're just like every character I've ever written about," she murmured.

"You do horror stories too?" I said.

Her lips moved closer to his. "Tim…"

"Charlotte…"

"The train's slowing down!" She broke free – and it was true. The train had slowed down while we were talking and now it had stopped completely. But we weren't in a station. We were in the middle of a field.

"I wonder…" she began. She got out of her seat and went over to the section between our carriage and the next. This was the only part of the train where there was a window you could open. I watched as she opened it and stuck her head out.

At the same time, the train started up again and quickly picked up speed.

When Charlotte came back, she looked worried. "It was a police block," she said. "Five of them just got on the train."

Sure enough, as the train continued, we

passed a police car parked next to the track. We were sitting right in the middle of the train. The policemen had got on at the front. I guessed it would take them less than a minute to reach us.

"How did they know you were on the train?" Charlotte asked.

"I don't know," Tim replied.

But I did. He had asked a policeman for directions at Victoria Station. The policeman must have followed us and seen us get onto the train.

"You're going to have to jump!" Charlotte said.

"Jump...?" I looked out of the window. We were already doing twenty miles per hour and moving faster by the second.

"Quickly!"

"Can we pull the communications cord first?" Tim asked.

"No." Charlotte shook her head. She'd already got it all worked out. A typical writer. "If you pull the cord, it will tell the police you were here."

"And there's a fifty pound fine," I added.

"Move!"

Still chained together, Tim and I got out of our seats and moved to the nearest door. Charlotte followed. Fortunately there were only a couple of other passengers near us and they were so buried in their papers that they didn't see us go.

We reached the nearest exit door. Tim pulled it open and stood there with the wind buffeting his face. The train was moving very fast now and I could see he had changed his mind about the plan. To be honest, I wasn't too wild about it either.

"Good luck," Charlotte said.

"Actually…" Tim began.

"Goodbye!" Charlotte said.

Tim fell out of the train and in that split second I realized two things: one – that Charlotte had given him a helpful push; and two – that I was still chained to him. With a yell I launched myself after him.

I felt the wind grab me. For a moment everything was a blur. Then long grass rushed up at me from all sides. I heard Tim yell, the sound blending in with the roar of the train. I could feel his weight at the end of the chain, still pulling me forward. There was a sickening thud as my shoulder came into contact with the earth. And then everything was blue, green, blue, green as I rolled down a hill between the grass and the sky. I couldn't see Tim any more and wondered if he'd managed to pull off my arm.

Then I must have blacked out for a moment. The next thing I knew, I was lying on my back, winded and only half-conscious. A pair of eyes that I thought I knew well loomed over me.

"Tim?" I muttered.

"Moo," came the reply. It was a cow. And it seemed as astonished as I was that I was still alive.

I raised my hand and was grateful to see it was still there. It seemed that I hadn't broken any bones in the fall – but I had broken the handcuffs. A length of chain trailed away from my wrist.

There was a loud groan a short distance away and Tim popped up behind a small bush. It had been a big bush until he had rolled through it. Tim had been less fortunate than me. As soon as we were separated, he had rolled through six nettles, a clump of thistles, a cowpat and the bush.

"Next time, we take a bus!" he muttered as I tried to tidy him up. The cow ambled over and tried to eat his sleeve. "Shoo!" Tim cried out. The cow put its head down to the ground and took a bite out of one of his shoes.

We chased the cow away and found Tim's other shoe. A few minutes later we crossed the field leaving the railway line behind us. There was a gap in the hedge and a lane on the other side. We turned left, following our noses. Actually, Tim's nose had been stung so badly, it now pointed both ways.

But he didn't complain. He was limping along beside me, deep in thought. For a long time neither of us spoke. Then, at last, he sighed. "Charlotte!" I'd had a feeling he was thinking about her. "You know, I really think she likes me."

I shrugged. "Well, she was certainly smiling when she pushed you off the train."

We reached a crossroads. This time there was a sign. Dover straight ahead. But it didn't say how far.

"How far do you think it is?" Tim asked.

"It can't be more than a couple of kilometres," I said. Tim grimaced. "I'm not sure I can make it, kid. I think I've twisted both my ankles."

I looked down. "No you haven't," I said. "You've got your shoes on the wrong feet."

"Oh."

We walked a little further and suddenly there we were. We were high up with the sea – a brilliant blue – below us. The port of Dover was a knotted fist with a ferry and a hovercraft slipping through its concrete fingers even as we watched. And to our left and to our right, as far as we could see, a ribbon of white stretched out beneath the sun. The White Cliffs of Dover. We had made it to the edge of England. But now we had to go further, over the water and away from home.

We slipped into the crowded port without being noticed. Maybe the police were still waiting for us at the station. Maybe they had given up on us and gone. There was a ferry leaving for Ostend in ten minutes. We took it. Despite what I'd been able to save from the bank robbery, we were getting low on cash so we only bought one-way tickets.

But as I said to Tim, if we didn't find Charon in Amsterdam, it was unlikely that we would be coming back.

THE SECRET AGENT

To be honest, I'm not crazy about Amsterdam. It's got too many canals, too many tourists and most of its buildings look like they've been built with a Lego set that's missing half its pieces. Also, the Dutch put mayonnaise on their chips. But if you like bicycles and cobbled streets, flower stalls and churches, I suppose there are worse places you can go.

We arrived the next morning after hitch-hiking up from Ostend. That was one good thing about Amsterdam. After three hours with a lorry driver, a cheese salesman and a professional juggler (who dropped us in the middle of the city) we realized that just about everyone in the place spoke English. This was just as well. Ten minutes after we'd set off in search of the Amstel Ijsbaan, we were hope-lessly lost. It wasn't just that we couldn't understand the street signs. We couldn't even pronounce them. We found our way by asking people. Not that that was much help.

Me: "Excuse me. We're looking for the Amstel Ijsbaan."

Friendly local: "Go along the canal. Turn left at the canal. Continue until you see a canal. And it's on a canal."

There were hundreds of canals and they all looked exactly the same. In fact if you went on holiday in Amsterdam you'd only need to take one photograph. Then you could develop it a few dozen times. We must have walked for an hour and a half before we finally found what we were looking for; a low, square building on the very edge of the city, stretching out into the only open space we'd seen. Like the rest of the place, the sign was old and needed repair. It read: AMS EL IJSBAAN.

"There's no 'T'," I said.

"That's all right," Tim muttered. "I'm not thirsty."

We went in. An old crone was sitting behind the glass window of the ticket office. Either she had a bad skin disease or the window needed cleaning. As Tim went over to her she put down the grubby paperback she had been reading and looked up at him with suspicious eyes.

"*Kan ik u misschien helpen?*" she said. It sounded like she was gargling, but that's the Dutch language for you. Tim stared at her.

"*Hoeveel kaartjes wilt u?*" she demanded more angrily.

You didn't have to be Einstein to work out what she was saying. After all, she was a ticket-seller and we needed tickets. But Tim just stood there, rooted to the spot, mumbling in what sounded like GCSE French. I stepped forward.

"*Twee kaarties alstublieft,*" I said and slid some money under the window. The old woman grunted, gave us two tickets and went back to her book.

"What did you say?" Tim demanded.

"I asked for two tickets."

"But when did you learn to speak Dutch?"

"On the ferry. I looked in a phrase book."

Tim's face lit up. "You're brilliant, Nick!"

"Not really." I shrugged. "It's just a phrase I'm going through."

We passed through a set of double doors. We could hear the ice rink in the distance now, or at least the music booming out over the speakers.

I noticed that Tim had picked up a pair of skates.

"We're here to look for 86," I reminded him. "We're not going skating."

"86 could be on the ice," he said.

"But Tim ... can you skate?"

"Can I skate?" He grinned at me. "*Can* I skate!"

Tim couldn't skate. I watched him fall over three times – and that was before he even reached the ice. Then I left him and began to search for the secret agent who called himself 86. How would I recognize him? He was hardly likely to have a badge with the number on it. A tattoo, perhaps? I decided to look out for anyone who seemed strange or out-of-place. The trouble was, in a run-down Dutch skating rink in the middle of the summer, *everyone* seemed out of place.

The ice rink was enormous. It was like being inside an aircraft hangar. It was rectangular in shape, surrounded by five rows of plastic seats rising in steps over the ice. There was an observation box at one end and the terrace café at the other. Everything was slightly shabby, old-fashioned ... and cold. The ice was actually steaming as it caught the warm air from outside and chilled it. There were only about half a dozen skaters out there and, as they glided along the surface of the rink, they seemed to disappear into the fog like bizarre, dancing ghosts.

There was also a handful of spectators. An old lady sat knitting. She might have been aged eighty-six but I somehow doubted that she was the agent. An ice-cream seller was sitting on his own, looking depressed because nobody was buying his ice creams. The nearest he got to eighty-six was the 99-flakes he was advertising.

I glanced back at Tim. He had fallen over again. Either that, or he was trying to ice-skate on his nose.

But there was one good skater on the ice, a real professional in a black tracksuit. If you've ever watched ice-skaters, you'll know that they seem to move without even trying. It's almost as though they're flying standing up. Well, this man was like that. I watched him as he sped round in a huge figure of eight. Then I turned back and began to thread my way through the remaining spectators.

That was when I saw them. They were sitting down in the middle of the highest row of seats with their legs spread out on the seats below them. One was tall and thin, dressed in a grey suit with a bow tie. At some time in his life he'd had a nasty argument with someone … and I mean nasty. The someone had left a scar that started just to the side of his left eye and ran all the way down to his neck. I'd never seen a scar quite like it. It looked like you could post a letter in it. His companion was shorter, dressed in jeans, white T-shirt and black leather jacket. He had hair like an oil-slick and a face that seemed to have been moulded by somebody with large thumbs. He didn't need a scar. He was ugly enough already.

Why had I noticed them? It was simple.

They weren't watching the ice. I got the feeling they were watching me – and as I walked past them, following a line of seats a few rows below, I felt their four eyes swivelling round and sticking to me like leeches in a swamp. Even as I went, I wondered if one of them could be Agent 86. But I didn't ask. I didn't want to know.

The music changed from classical to jazz.

Tim fell over more jazzily this time. The professional swung round him in another smooth circle. Scarface and Ugly were still sitting where I'd seen them, only now they were looking away. I decided to ignore them.

But where was 86?

I walked up to the top row, passing seat eighty-six as I went. It was empty. I turned back and took one last look at the rink. Tim was sitting on the ice, shaking his head, and suddenly I wanted to laugh. The man in the black tracksuit had skated two figures round him. I could see the figures cut by the blades in the surface of the ice. An eight and a six.

I ran back down to the edge of the rink and called to Tim. That was a mistake. I'd allowed myself to get excited and I'd shown it. And although I only half-noticed it then, I had good reason to remember it later.

Scarface and Ugly were watching me again.

*   *   *

We found the tracksuit in the changing room but the skater was no longer in it. He was taking a shower. We waited until he came out, a white towel wrapped round his waist. He was a tough, broad-shouldered man. The water was still glistening off muscles that would have looked good on a horse. He had pale skin and grey, watchful eyes that reminded me of my old friend Inspector Snape. He sat down between Tim and me without seeming to notice either of us.

"86?" I said.

He just sat there as if he hadn't even heard me. Then slowly he turned his head and looked at me with an expressionless face. "I don't know you," he said.

Tim took over. "I liked the skating," he said. "You always practise figures?"

The skater shrugged. "What of it?" His English was almost perfect, but with a slight American accent.

"I'm a friend of a friend of yours," Tim explained. "A guy called McMuffin."

"McGuffin," I corrected him.

The skater shook his head. Water dripped out of his hair. "I don't know this name…"

Tim smiled. He was playing the private detective now – cooler than the ice on the rink. "Well, here's something else you don't know," he drawled. "McGuffin is in his McCoffin."

The skater seemed uninterested. "Who are

you?" he demanded.

"The name's Tim Diamond. Private eye."

"How about you?" I asked.

"My name is Rushmore. Hugo Rushmore. I'm sorry to hear about your friend but I can't help you. I'm just a skater. That's all."

For a moment I almost believed him – but the figures cut in the ice couldn't have been just a coincidence. And without Agent 86, we were nowhere.

I decided to have one last try. "Please, Mr Rushmore," I said. "You've got to help us."

Still he looked blank. And then I remembered the ticket that I had found in McGuffin's hotel room, the ticket that had brought us all this way. I still had it in my pocket. I fished it out and handed it to him.

"McGuffin gave us this," I said. "Before he died."

Rushmore took the ticket. It was as if I'd said the right password or turned on some sort of switch. A light came on in his eyes. "All right," he said. "Let's get a drink."

We went up to the café terrace I'd seen before. It had a view over the rink, but either the day had got warmer or the ice had got colder, because there was so much mist you could hardly see it.

I could just make out two figures standing at the far end and thought of Scarface and Ugly but they were too far away and the mist washed them out. Rushmore was drinking a Coke and had bought us both milk shakes, which would have been nicer if someone had remembered to shake the milk.

"There's not a lot I can tell you," he began. "I do a little work for the Dutch Secret Service..."

"What sort of work?" Tim asked.

"That's a secret. But I'll tell you this much. I was ordered to look after Jake McGuffin while he was over here. His boss – Mr Waverly – was desperate to find Charon." Rushmore paused and considered. "There was something odd going on," he added. "Something Waverly hadn't told Jake."

"You mean, Waverly was keeping something back?" I said.

"That's right. There was a connection between Mr Waverly and Charon. It was as if they knew each other in some way. Jake said the whole thing stank. But he never found out what it was..."

A connection between Waverly and Charon. It seemed impossible. After all, Waverly was the one who wanted to find Charon. It was all getting confusing. "What was McGuffin doing here in Holland?" I asked.

"He'd followed Charon over here." Rushmore finished his Coke. "The last time I saw

93

him he was planning to check out some old house just outside the city."

"You know the name?" Tim asked.

Rushmore nodded. "Yes. It's called the Winter House. The *Villa de Winter*, in Dutch. It's about twenty kilometres from Amsterdam."

"Twenty kilometres..." Tim tried to work it out on his fingers. He didn't have enough fingers.

"Twelve miles," I said. I turned to Rushmore. "Could you take us there?"

His eyes narrowed. "It could be dangerous."

"That's all right," Tim chimed in. "You can go in first."

Rushmore looked from Tim back to me. "All right," he said. "The rink closes at six today. Come back at five past. I'll drive you out this evening."

We stood up.

"See you later, Mr Skater," I muttered.

"Yeah. Watch how you go, Hugo," Tim added. I looked down at the ice, searching for the figures that I'd glimpsed behind the mist. But the ice was empty. The two of them had gone.

We got back to the ice rink at six o'clock after an afternoon in Amsterdam. It was still light outside, but once we'd passed through the swing doors into the old building it was as if we'd entered some sort of artificial Arctic night. The ticket-seller had gone home. The lights had been turned off and the windows with their frosted glass and wire grills kept most of the sunlight out. The rink itself stretched out silent and empty, with the mist still curling gently on the surface. The music was switched off, too. But the machine that made the ice was still active. I could hear it humming and hissing like some sort of mythical creature, its pipes spreading out like tentacles, chilling everything they touched.

"Where is he?" I whispered. My words were taken by the cold air and sent scurrying up towards the rafters. *Where is he? Where is he?*

I could almost hear the echo.

The mist on the ice folded over itself, rolling towards us.

"What...?" Tim began.

There was something on the ice. It was in the very middle, a grey bundle that could have been somebody's old clothes.

"Wait here," I said.

I walked through the barrier and onto the ice. I could feel it, cold underneath my shoes. As I walked forward, my feet slid away from under me and I had to struggle to stay upright. The ice-making pipes rumbled softly below. The mist swirled round my ankles, clinging to my skin. I wanted to hurry but I was forced to be slow.

At last I reached the bundle.

It was Rushmore. The Dutch secret agent must have been on his way to meet us, crossing the ice when he was stopped. Somebody had found out who he was and had known about his connection with McGuffin. And they had made sure that he wouldn't help us.

He had been stabbed twice. The blades were still in his back, one between his shoulders, the other just above his waist. There was a pool of blood around his outstretched hand. It had already frozen solid.

I took one last look at the body and at the blades, long and silver and horribly appropriate. Because whoever had killed Hugo Rushmore, professional ice-skater and spy, hadn't used knives.

They'd used a pair of ice-skating boots.

SHREDDED WHEAT

We spent the night at a cheap motel on the edge of Amsterdam. Our money was low and so were we. Rushmore had been our only link in a chain that might lead us to Charon and now he was dead. Worse still, it seemed that Charon knew we were in Amsterdam. How else could he have got to the ice-rink before us?

It was raining when we got to the Van Bates Motel. We were shown to our room by a thin, twitchy manager who didn't speak a word of English. In the end we had to get his mother down to translate.

All I wanted was a shower and a bed but the shower wasn't working and as usual Tim took the bed. There was a TV in one corner of the room. It was tuned to the BBC – the ten o'clock news. I didn't want to hear the news but I was somehow glad to hear another English voice. I listened. And suddenly I was glad I'd turned it on.

There was a reporter on the screen. He was standing outside Sotheby's, the auction house in New Bond Street, London.

"Boris Kusenov—" They were the first two words I'd heard. That was what had caught my attention— "is considered to be the key figure in the struggle for power at the Kremlin."

The picture changed. Now the reporter was inside the auction house, standing in front of a large canvas. For a moment I thought the TV had broken. Then I realized. This was modern art.

"Kusenov is in England to bid for a canvas by the surrealist painter, Salvador Dali," the reporter's voice went on. "Titled 'The Tsar's Feast', it depicts Tsar Nicholas II offering stale bread to his dissatisfied serfs…"

Well, that may have been what it looked like to him. To me the picture looked like a bent watch beside a pink lake being examined by two oversized amoebas. Had Kusenov come all the way from Russia just to buy this? The TV screen cut to a picture of the reporter. He answered the question for me.

"Kusenov came to Britain unexpectedly because of his belief that the painting should hang in Russia. Although it is expected to reach almost a million pounds, he will be bidding for it when it is auctioned at Sotheby's in two days' time."

The reporter smirked at the camera and the programme cut back to the studio and the next news item.

"Police have completely lost the track of the dangerous criminal, Tim Diamond, who…"

I turned the set off. I'd heard quite enough about *him*.

"Kusenov," I muttered. Tim was sitting upright on the bed. The sound of his own name had evidently woken him up. "He's already in England."

"Is that bad?" Tim asked.

I sighed. It wasn't bad. It was terrible. "It means we're running out of time. Charon could move at any moment." I thought for a minute. "We've got to find this Winter House," I said. "We need help."

Tim's eyes lit up. "Charlotte!"

"You'd better call her."

Tim called her. The phone rang about six times before we were connected. Charlotte answered in Dutch.

"Charlotte?" Tim interrupted. "It's me … Tim."

"Tim?" There was a pause and I wondered if she'd forgotten who he was. But then she continued breathlessly. "Thank goodness you rang. I have to see you. I think I've found something."

"What?" Tim asked.

"I can't tell you. Not over the telephone. Let's meet somewhere safe." Another pause. I could hear heavy breathing. It took me a few seconds to realize it was Tim's. Then Charlotte cut in again. "Just outside Amsterdam, in the Flavoland. There's a crossroads and a bus stop. Can you meet me there tomorrow morning? At nine."

"Tomorrow?" Tim crooned. "But that's a whole day away!"

"I know."

"I'll be there."

Tim hung up. "Tomorrow," he said. "Just off the Flavobahn. In Autoland."

"I heard," I said.

And I had heard. Charlotte was frightened and Rushmore was dead. Charon, it seemed, was everywhere. How long would it be before he moved in on us?

Take a bus north out of Amsterdam and after a while you'll come to the Flavoland. When you look for a view and find you haven't got one, that's when you'll know you're there. The Flavoland used to be the bottom of the sea until someone had the bright idea of taking the water away. What was left was a great, flat, wide, empty nothing. Dutch farmers use it to grow their crops in, and that's all there is: fields of corn, wheat, barley and maize stretching out to a horizon as regular as a plate. There isn't one hill in the Flavoland. There are no trees. And the birds are too bored to whistle.

There was only one bus stop in the area and it was right next to the crossroads that Charlotte had described. The bus-driver tried to stop us getting out – he must have thought we were crazy – but we insisted.

"When does the next bus arrive?" I asked.

"Tomorrow," he replied.

And then it was gone, kicking up a cloud of dust, and we were alone with the wind and the wheat.

Really alone.

I looked behind me. Nothing. I looked ahead. Nothing. The road was just two lines that ran together and the bus was already a speck at the far end. The wheat rippled gently in the breeze. It was a hot day. The sun was beating down and with no hills and no trees there were no shadows. We were in the middle of a giant frying pan. And there was no sign of Charlotte.

Tim looked at his watch. "She's late."

I could hear a faint droning. At first I thought it was a wasp. Out of the corner of my eye I saw something small passing in front of the sun. But it wasn't an insect. It was a plane, spraying the crops about two or three kilometres to the south. I watched as it flew in a straight line, parallel to the horizon. I could see it more clearly now, an old wooden

101

propeller plane with two sets of wings on each side, like something out of the First World War. It was leaving a silvery cloud behind it, thin drops of pesticide or something drifting down onto...

"That's funny," I said.

"What's that?" Tim asked.

"That plane's dusting crops where there ain't no crops."

The plane turned sharply and began to fly towards us. I could hear the propeller chopping at the air. The engine sounded angry. For a long time I just stood there watching it. Maybe it was the heat. Maybe I was tired. I didn't realize I was watching my own death.

But then the plane swooped down and before my brain had time to tell me what was going on my legs were hurling me out of the way as the whole thing sliced through the air millimetres above where my head had just been. Tim shrieked and threw himself in the other direction. For a moment everything went dark as the plane blotted out the sun. The propeller whipped up the surface of the road, stinging my eyes. And then it was gone, climbing upwards and at the same time turning for the next attack.

Tim got to his knees, coughing and blinking. I don't think he'd quite understood what was happening. "Low flying..." he muttered.

I nodded. "Any lower and it wouldn't need wings."

102

"Do you think…?"

But even Tim had worked out what I was thinking. It was Charon. Somehow he had found out about our meeting with Charlotte.

I remembered now how scared she'd been on the telephone. Maybe she'd been followed. Maybe she was already dead.

Charon was up there. And we had nowhere to run, nowhere to hide. Because that was exactly where we were. Nowhere.

I was still wondering which way to run when the plane swept down again. And this time there was an even more unpleasant surprise. Two of its wings were fitted with machine-guns. I saw the sparks of red and heard the chatter of the bullets. A section of the road leaped up at me, the tarmac shattering. Tim dived to one side and I tried to follow him but then something punched me hard on the shoulder and I was thrown on my back. The plane rushed past, the wind battering and blinding me. I knew I had been hit but I didn't know how badly. I was hurting all over.

But then the plane had gone and somehow I had got to my feet. I looked round for Tim. His face was white but it could have been dust. The plane was banking steeply, preparing for the next attack. Third time lucky…?

We only had one chance. "Come on!" I shouted. "The wheat!"

"I can't!" Tim was frozen. The plane had almost completed its turn.

"Why not?"

"My hay fever...!"

"Tim!" It was incredible. Charon had us right in his sights and Tim was worrying about his hay fever. Any minute now he'd have more holes in him than a Swiss cheese and the next time he sneezed, he'd do it in fourteen directions at once. But this was no time to argue. Ignoring the pain in my shoulder, I grabbed hold of him and pushed him off the road.

The plane dived again, invisible this time, and a great patch of wheat tore itself apart spectacularly around me. Tim sneezed. At least he hadn't been hit. But this was hopeless. We could stumble through the field until the whole thing looked like a plate of cornflakes but we'd end up as the free gifts in the middle. Eventually Charon would pick us off. We had to do something. Now.

And then I saw them. They'd been left in the middle of the wheat and they had both fallen over into a sad and useless heap. They were made of wire and old broomstick handles with punctured footballs for heads. Scarecrows. Even the most cowardly of crows wouldn't have been scared by them but they'd given me an idea.

I searched for the plane. It was at its furthest point, turning again. Then I yelled at Tim.

"Take off your jacket!"

"Why?"

"Just do it!"

I pulled off my own jacket. It hurt me and as my sleeve came free I saw that it was soaked in blood. But it would just have to wait. I grabbed hold of one of the scarecrows and threw it towards Tim. Miraculously he'd got the idea without my having to explain it. We had no time. The plane had almost completed its turn, a shimmering dot in the face of the sun. I hoped that Charon would be blinded by the glare, that he wouldn't see what we were doing. I'd managed to get my jacket onto the smaller scarecrow. It hung off the wooden framework clumsily and the football face – black and white and half deflated – looked nothing like mine. At least, I hope it didn't. I glanced back. The plane had completed its turn. It was coming at us, out of the sun.

"Tim…?"

He'd hung his own jacket onto the other scarecrow. Carefully, we leaned them against each other, shoulder to shoulder. They swayed but stood upright like two drunken friends. The noise of the plane reached me and I almost felt the wheat shiver behind me.

"Duck!" I shouted.

We threw ourselves into the wheat at the same moment as the bullets erupted again. I looked up and saw the two scarecrows only a metre or two away cut in half by the scythe of gunfire. The plane roared overhead. And then it was all over. The plane continued the way it had come, disappearing in the distance. The scarecrows lay in tatters on a bed of shredded wheat. The wind stroked the rest of the crop as if trying to soothe it after what had happened.

We stood up. We wouldn't be wearing our jackets again. The bullets had turned them into so many handkerchiefs. Tim gazed up at the sky, "You think it was Charon?" he said.

"Who else could it have been?" I replied.

"A farmer…"

"What? Using machine-gun bullets to spray the crops?"

Tim considered. "Maybe it was an organic farmer."

I shook my head. "I don't think so."

There was a long silence. I found I was unconsciously gripping my arm. I could feel the blood seeping through my fingers.

Tim was deep in thought. At last he spoke. "If it was Charon," he muttered, "he'll think we're dead now. And if he thinks we're dead, he won't try and kill us."

"Right," I agreed.

Tim brightened. "Well, I suppose that's a shot in the arm." Then he saw the blood.

"Nick!"

"What?"

"You've been shot in the arm."

"I know."

Tim took a step forward. His face had gone a cheesy-white and I knew what was about to happen. And a moment later it did. With a little moan, he crumpled and joined the two scarecrows, stretched out in the heat. He never had been able to stand the sight of blood.

I just stood where I was, clutching my arm. It was hurting more now, but that was good. It reminded me that I was still alive.

CHARON

"Now, this won't hurt..."

Why do doctors always say that before they hurt you?

Dr Monika Bloem wasn't even a doctor. She was a vet. We'd found her farmhouse just outside the Flavoland as we'd walked back towards the city. I wasn't too happy about being treated by someone who was more comfortable with dogs and rabbits, but I didn't have much choice. I'd left about half a litre of my blood in a dotted line along the road and although it may have looked pretty, I didn't have enough to continue it all the way to Amsterdam.

Dr Bloem (it rhymed with "room") was a short, serious woman in a white coat. She had a neat clinic lined with cages of various sizes, and it was easy to see that she was married to her work. Her best man had probably been a goat.

There were pictures of animals everywhere – even in the frames on her desk. She had only agreed reluctantly to treat a human being. And she had fed me two lumps of sugar first.

Sure enough there was a moment of excruciating pain as she probed my wound with a pair of tweezers but then she was backing away with a red, glistening bullet firmly trapped between the prongs.

"You are feeling all right?" she asked. Her English was accented, not as good as her surgical skills.

"Well, I'm still a bit faint…" Tim began.

She glared at him. "I mean your brother."

I flexed my arm. "I'm OK, Dr Bloem," I said.

"You are lucky, I think." The doctor dropped the bullet into a kidney tray. It hit the bottom with a dull clang. "A centimetre to the left and it would have hit an artery."

"Yeah," Tim agreed. "And it could have been worse. A centimetre to the right and it would have hit me!"

Dr Bloem unwrapped a packet of bandages. "You know, I think you are not telling me the truth," she said as she did it. "How did the bullet get into the arm?"

"Well…" I began. This was tricky. We hadn't had time to make up a sensible explanation and our story – like my arm – was full of holes.

"Your brother said you were hurt in a car accident," Dr Bloem went on.

"It's true!" Tim explained. "It was the driver of the car."

"Yes," I added. "He accidentally shot me."

Dr Bloem didn't believe us but she wrapped the bandage round my arm and tied a knot. "It is finished," she said. "You should be OK now."

"Thanks, Doc." I tried the arm again. It was throbbing but most of the pain had gone.

"So how will the two of you get back to town?" Dr Bloem asked. "I would take you but I have another patient. He's a little horse."

"Has he tried gargling?" Tim said.

Dr Bloem ignored him. "You can walk – but it's a long way. So maybe you should ask for a ride. There's a big house just one kilometre up the road. Near a windmill."

"What's it called?" I asked.

Dr Bloem smiled at me. "It's called the *Villa de Winter*," she said. "The Winter House."

I'd never seen a house quite like the Winter House. It was built out of red and white bricks but not with any pattern. The colours seemed to zigzag across the walls, colliding with each other, then bouncing away again. The whole building could have been put together by a thief. The towers had been stolen from a

110

castle, the windows from a church, the grey slate roof from a railway station.

The house was set back from the road. Tim and I had climbed over a fence to get in and we were squatting some distance from the building itself, spying on it through a bush.

"Do you think this is where Charon lives?" Tim asked.

I nodded. "This is where McGuffin came before he was killed."

"Right." Tim gazed at the house. "If only we could see through the wall."

"We can!" I said.

"How?"

"The window..."

We broke cover and sprinted across the lawn to the side of the house. Our shadows reached it first. There was nobody in sight, but now I could hear the sound of a piano drifting out of one of the windows. I recognized the music – but only just. It was Beethoven's "Moonlight Sonata", but played very badly. It occurred to me that the pianist might be missing a finger.

"Listen!" I nudged Tim.

"Is it a record?" Tim asked.

"Yes. Nobody's ever played it that badly."

Tim's mouth dropped open. "Charon!"

"It figures. He killed McGuffin. And now he's murdering Beethoven."

We had both been crouching down but now

I straightened up and tried to lever myself onto the window sill above me. Tim was horrified. "What are you doing?"

"It could be our only chance to see what Charon looks like," I said.

And it could have been. But just as my fingers grabbed hold of the woodwork I heard a car. It was coming up the drive, heading for the main entrance. I dropped down again and squatted next to Tim. At the same time the piano playing stopped and I heard a door close. There were two dustbins just beside us. I edged closer to them, using them to hide behind.

The car had stopped. Two men got out. I recognized them, although I had only seen them once before. They had faces you were unlikely to forget. Scarface and Ugly – the two men from the skating-rink. The gravel crunched under their feet as they walked towards the door. The noise made me think of the skates in Rushmore's back, and I swallowed hard.

Tim was staring after them. I tugged at his sleeve. "Let's go in," I whispered.

He opened his mouth to argue but I didn't give him time. There was a door just on the other side of the window and, for once, luck was on our side – it was open. Making sure that Tim was still following me, I went in, up a short flight of steps and into a corridor paved with black and white tiles – like in one of those old Dutch paintings. The corridor must have led into a hall. I could hear voices in the distance, the two guests being welcomed. There was another door on our left. It opened into a large room with a desk, four or five antique chairs and a grand piano. It had to be Charon's room. I slid across the polished floor and found my feet on a Chinese rug.

"What are we doing?" Tim hissed.

What *were* we doing? Already I could hear the rap of footsteps making their way back along the corridor. Charon was about to come in with his two friends. If they found us there, I doubted they'd invite us to stay for tea…

"Quick!" There was an alcove to one side, half-covered by a heavy, ornamental curtain. We ran behind it and pulled it the whole way across. A second later, Charon and the two new arrivals walked in.

I heard them close the door and come into the room. Someone was talking in rapid Dutch. I couldn't understand a word of it, nor did I recognize the voice. A second person spoke. I didn't recognize his voice either. But this time I did understand one word of it. The name Waverly. Why were they talking about the head of MI6? Rushmore had told us that there was some sort of secret connection between them. Was that what they were discussing now?

It was infuriating. I was stuck behind the curtain with Tim. I couldn't understand a word that was being spoken. And I couldn't see anything either. Why had we even bothered to come in? I glanced at Tim. There was a tiny chink of light on one side of his cheek. I followed it back to the curtain. The curtain was torn! I hadn't noticed it before but there was a small hole, right in the middle. I leaned forward and put my eye against it, trying not to move the material. I could feel my heart pounding against my chest. At last I was going to see Charon!

But it wasn't to be. Charon had chosen the antique chair that had its back to the curtain. Looking through the hole I could see Scarface, smoking a cigarette in the chair opposite him, and Ugly, standing to one side. But Charon was concealed.

And then he spoke. It was a single word and I didn't understand it, but at least I had heard his voice. It was a chesty sort of voice, not deep. Had I heard it somewhere before?

His hand stretched out and I saw the four fingers open in a palm-up gesture. At the same time, Ugly hurried forward with a small white hammer. It was another antique, probably made of ivory. What were they doing with it? Ugly jabbered away for about one minute and I got the sense that they were wrapping things up. If only Charon would stand up … every

114

nerve in my body was screaming at him to get out of the chair.

It was Scarface who got to his feet. He walked across towards the curtain and I was forced to retreat from the eyehole, away into the shadow. There were more mutterings behind him. The door opened and I knew even without looking that Charon was on his way out. Sure enough, when the door closed, the room was silent. I had been that close to unravelling the biggest mystery of all. But not quite close enough.

"Have they gone?" Tim whispered.

"They've gone…" I pushed back the curtain and went out into the room. Charon might have left but his desk was still there. I just hoped he didn't lock his drawer.

"Did you see his face?" Tim asked.

"No. But I heard a bit of what they said. They were talking about Mr Waverly."

I pulled open the top drawer. I'm not sure what I was looking for. Would Charon have a driving licence, a photograph of himself, a credit card?

Surely there would be something to tell me who he was? But the drawer was empty apart from three paperclips, a comb, a small mirror covered in some sort of powder and a half-smoked packet of cigarettes.

It told me nothing. I wasn't thinking. It should have told me who Charon was.

I tried the second drawer. And that was where I found it. It was an ordinary cheque, made out for the sum of four hundred thousand guilders. Payable to "Charon Enterprises". And signed by...

I showed it to Tim. "Four hundred thousand guilders!" he exclaimed. "That's..." But as usual his mathematics wouldn't stretch that far.

"It's about £120,000," I said. "But look at the signature."

Tim read it. His eyes bulged. "Mr Waverly!"

"That's right," I said. "Mr Waverly is the one who's paying Charon to kill Kusenov."

"But why?" Tim demanded. "He was the one who wanted to *stop* Charon."

"I know." I pocketed the cheque. None of it made any sense – but at least I had some sort of evidence against Waverly. "Come on." I moved towards the door. "Let's get out of here."

"Let's take the window," Tim said, moving the other way.

"And keep it quiet. OK?"

He opened the window. Alarm bells exploded throughout the house.

It was too late to argue now. We dived head first through the window together, hit the grass in a somersault and staggered to our feet. A door crashed open behind us and I glimpsed

Scarface hurtling towards us. But I was already halfway across the lawn, running with all my strength towards the undergrowth that might offer somewhere to hide. There was a bang and something whizzed past my head. My arm was suddenly hurting again. Hadn't I been shot at enough for one day?

We jumped over the first shrubs and sprinted on through the rough woodland at the edge of the house. Ugly had joined Scarface. I heard him shout something in Dutch. There was a second shot. Tim screamed. I wheeled round.

"Are you hit?" I demanded.

"No. I stepped on a stinging nettle."

"We've got to find the road."

We found the road about thirty seconds before Scarface and Ugly found us. Even as we climbed over the fence and dropped down on to the tarmac, the wood was torn to splinters by another burst of gunfire. But there were no cars on the road. No buses. Nothing. We still hadn't got away.

"Where now?" Tim panted.

"There!"

Dr Bloem had said the Winter House was near a windmill and there it was, a few hundred metres away, its huge sails turning slowly in the wind.

It was our only hope. We had nowhere else to hide and I knew that Scarface and Ugly would be over the fence – or perhaps through it – in seconds. With Tim close behind me I crossed the road. There was only one door and it was open.

One way in. One way out. It was only when I was inside that I realized we were trapped. Worse still, Scarface and Ugly had seen us go in. I saw them now, guns in their hands, slowly crossing the road towards us. Scarface was smiling. It made his scar bend in the middle so that it was like the point of an arrow. And the arrow was pointing at me.

"They're coming after us!" Tim was close to panic. "What are we going to do?"

"Hide!"

Tim went one way. I went another.

The inside of the windmill was like nothing I'd imagined. In fact it seemed bigger inside than out with a mass of slowly turning wooden beams, wheels and great stones all meshing together like the workings of some fantastic clock. Four separate staircases ran up in different directions. One led to a door that opened on to an outer gallery, and this was the one I chose. I felt trapped inside the mill. If anybody was going to shoot me, I'd prefer it to be in the open.

I scrabbled up the staircase – it was more like a ladder – wondering which way Tim would go. But I didn't have time to worry about him. Even as I reached the top and the sunlight, I saw Scarface grab the bottom of the ladder and start up. Maybe fifteen seconds separated us. I had to find somewhere to hide.

But where? I was on a narrow wooden platform that circled all the way round the windmill about four metres above the ground ... too high to jump. There were no other doors. I could run round and round in circles. But there was no other way up and the way back was blocked. A great shadow swept over me as one of the sails sliced down, cutting diagonally across the platform.

The sail...

I knew it was a crazy idea even as I started moving towards it. If you think a windmill's sails are slow and gentle, think again. Even when the wind is down they move at speed and they're strong enough to stun an ox. I was just lucky this wasn't a windy day.

As the next section of the sail swung round I leaped forward and grabbed it. Somehow my hands found the rough wooden framework behind the canvas. My arms were almost pulled out of their sockets. But an instant later, without any effort at all, I had been jerked off my feet and into the air, spinning round with the sail in an enormous, sickening, heart-stopping circle.

I clung on desperately. At the same time I kicked out with my feet and managed to find a grip between the wood and the canvas. I was left pinned to the sail – like a fly on flypaper as it spun me silently round and round, the green grass whirling away, the blue sky streaking in. It was as if the whole world were being stirred in a gigantic pot.

I shut my eyes. I couldn't watch.

But would Scarface see me? I could imagine him standing on the platform, circling it once, searching for me. Would he look up? I was behind the sail so unless he was standing at the back of the windmill I had to be hidden from him.

The windmill must have turned thirty times. I'd lost count after the fifteenth revolution. Everything I'd eaten in the last two days was threatening to leave my stomach. My arms and legs were groaning, feeling the weight of every turn. The wind dropped again. The sail slowed down. I'd had enough. As the platform veered up at me, I let go and fell in an untidy heap onto the hard wooden surface. If Scarface was still there, if he shot me now, it would only come as a relief.

But Scarface had already gone. I was too giddy to get to my feet but as I lay there, exhausted, I saw the assassins running across the fields below. They must have assumed I'd jumped down and got away. Then the nasty thought struck me.

Had they found Tim?

It was another five minutes before I found

the strength and the balance to get up. Even then the ladder down was a nightmare. I could still feel the motion of the sail inside my head and the ladder twisted away from me like a snake. It was ominously silent below. The only sound was the grinding of the massive stone as it turned in endless circles, crushing whatever got in the way into dust.

There was no sign of Tim.

Using my hands to keep myself upright, I staggered round the lower level. There were great sacks of flour to one side and, at the back, a loose heap of the stuff, stretching halfway up the wall. The platform above my head was empty. The door leading out was closed.

"Tim!" I shouted. "Where are you?"

Silence. I was starting to worry.

"Tim! It's all right! They've gone!"

Then something moved. I turned round. The loose flour, piled two metres high against the wall, was shifting. It was like watching a miniature avalanche.

A hand reached out, clawing at the air. The whole pile broke open and I was just able to make out a figure, fighting its way free. Flour was everywhere, billowing out into the air. Somehow Tim had managed to bury himself in it. Now he was free.

He stood there, completely white from head to foot. Maybe Ugly *had* shot him and this was his ghost.

"Hab day gob?" he asked.

There was flour in his nose and mouth. He sneezed. Flour cascaded out of his hair and a little pink circle appeared around his nose and mouth.

"Have they gone?" he tried again.

"Yeah. Are you all right?"

"I'm all white," Tim mumbled. At least, that's what it sounded like.

"Let's move."

We stalked out of the windmill, Tim leaving white footprints behind him. The sails were still turning slowly behind us.

In the last twelve hours we'd been machine-gunned through a cornfield and stitched up by a vet. We'd found Charon's headquarters and we'd come infuriatingly close to seeing Charon. We'd stolen Mr Waverly's cheque and we'd almost been shot getting away with it.

And now we were dead on our feet. We needed a bath and a long, long sleep. Because you had to admit – both of us had been through the mill.

STAGE FRIGHT

Twenty-four hours later we found ourselves on the platform of Central Station in Amsterdam. We'd paid our bill at the Van Bates Motel and bought two tickets to England. That was the end of our money. And here we were at the end of the line.

"I don't get it," Tim said. He'd managed to get rid of most of the flour but I noticed his hair was still a bit white at the sides. Maybe that was permanent. After the experiences of the last few days I wouldn't have been surprised. "I thought we weren't going back to England," he went on.

"We have to," I explained. "We've got to warn the Russian – Boris Kusenov. He can't trust Mr Waverly. Because it looks like Waverly is the one who is paying to get him killed."

"Right." Tim thought about it. "And he

can't trust anyone with hammers."

"Yeah. You tell him that."

But that was still a puzzle. We had seen Charon handling an antique white hammer. But what was he going to do with it? Bludgeon Kusenov to death?

And there was something else. South by south east. McGuffin's dying words. In all the excitement I had almost forgotten all about them. But we still hadn't found out what they meant.

"Nick!" Tim pointed.

It was the last person I'd expected to see. Charlotte Van Dam was walking along the platform, dressed in a light suit, carrying a handbag. I thought she was going to see us but at the last minute she forked off to the left and went into a smart café to one side.

"What's she doing here?" I muttered.

"She must be taking a train," Tim suggested.

"I know that," I said. "But where to? And why didn't she meet us in the wheatfield?"

Tim considered. "I don't know. Let's ask her."

"Yes. Let's ask."

The café at platform 2b resembled something out of an Agatha Christie novel, all wood panelling and marble bars with waiters in white aprons and tea that came in bone china, not plastic cups. Charlotte was sitting

124

by a window that looked back out over the platform towards the trains. A waiter was serving her with a cup of hot chocolate and a croissant that could have been a late lunch. It was two o'clock. Our train to Ostend left at twenty past.

We went over to her. She saw us and for a moment there was something in her eyes that wasn't exactly pleasure. It was there and then it was gone. She smiled and stood up.

"Tim!" she exclaimed. "I've been so worried about you!" She kissed him lightly on the cheek.

Tim blushed. "You have?"

"Of course I have. Ever since I read about that ice-skater getting killed..."

"Rushmore," I muttered.

"The late 86," Tim added.

"Yeah," I said. "They finally got his number."

Charlotte sat down and waved us both to a seat. "So tell me what's been happening to you," she said.

Tim shifted uncomfortably. "Charlotte," he began. "We went to the Flavoland like you said. But you never turned up."

She shook her head, guiltily. "I know. I couldn't."

"Why not?" I asked.

She looked up. "Oh Tim – Nick ... I've lied to you."

"I don't believe you!" Tim said.

"I have. You see … I'm not really a mystery writer."

Tim frowned. "What *do* you write then, Charlotte?"

"I don't write at all!" She took a deep breath.

"I'm a spy," she said. "I work for the Dutch Secret Service – like 86. I couldn't tell you before because I'm working undercover. You see, I'm on the track of Charon too."

"That still doesn't explain why you didn't meet us," I said.

"I was going to. But at the last minute I found I was being followed. There were two men. One of them had a scar."

"Short and ugly," Tim muttered.

"Yes. It was a short and ugly scar. I had to get away from them. But by the time I'd shaken them off, it was too late to come."

Tim turned to me. "You see," he said. "I told you there would be an explanation."

"How did the two of them get on to you?" I asked.

"I don't know. It's Charon. He seems to know everything I do before I do it. I can't move without…" She broke off. Her eyes were staring out of the window. "Oh my God!"

I twisted round. And suddenly I felt tired.

They hadn't seen us yet but Scarface and Ugly

were on the platform outside. And they were about to come in.

"It's them!" Charlotte whispered. She had stood up and the colour was draining from her face. "We've got to split up."

"Right." Tim turned to Charlotte. "I'll go with you."

"Thanks, Tim," I said.

But Charlotte was already moving away, making for the kitchens at the back. "No. You go your way. I'll go mine."

Tim opened his mouth to call after her. But she'd already gone.

She'd left her gloves on the table. I picked them up. They'd make a nice souvenir for Tim.

Then Scarface and Ugly arrived.

There were two exits from the restaurant. As they came in one, we went out the other. A staircase led down, away from the platform, right next to the restaurant. We took it. It looked like we'd just have to give the two-twenty Ostend train a miss.

The staircase took us down and out of the station. I didn't need to look to know that Scarface and Ugly were after us. I could hear the grunts and protests of innocent bystanders as they were brutally shoved out of the way.

"In here!" I shouted.

Tim didn't hear me. As I dived into a building on the other side of the road, I saw him disappear round the corner. We had split up

127

again, but maybe that was for the best. At least one of us might get away.

I skidded to a halt and looked around me. As I'd run in, I'd thought the building was a library or perhaps a museum. But now I saw that it was in fact a small, old-fashioned theatre. There was a ticket-office beside the door and a poster showing an old man in an evening suit. There were cards tumbling out of his hands and the name, Mr Marvano, written underneath. A magician – just what I needed. Maybe he could help me disappear.

The show had already begun. The ticket-seller was reading a newspaper and there were no ushers on the door. I tiptoed through the foyer and into the darkness of the auditorium. I just hoped Scarface and Ugly hadn't seen me go in.

Mr Marvano was standing on the stage, an old man with a round, pink face and silver hair, looking rather sad in his tails and white bow tie. As I came in he had just finished some sort of trick with a cane and a silk scarf. He had turned one of them into the other. There was a thin pattering of applause. Mr Marvano picked up a pack of playing-cards and began to explain the next trick in Dutch. I took a seat in the back row. There were plenty of empty seats.

It was cool inside the theatre. I could feel the perspiration beading on my face. I wondered how much of the show I would have to watch before it was safe to go out. It didn't make any sense. How had Scarface and Ugly managed to turn up at the station? Charlotte had said that Charon seemed to know everything she did – before she did it. How? In London, at the ice-rink and now in Amsterdam, Charon always seemed to be one step ahead.

There was more applause and I glanced at the stage. A Queen of Spades was rising, seemingly on its own, out of Mr Marvano's top pocket.

"Was this the card you picked?" the magician asked. He said it in Dutch but I understood anyway. I'd seen it, and heard it all, before.

Somebody appeared, walking down the aisle, and stopped at the end of my row. I looked round and froze. It was Scarface.

I half rose, planning to slide out the other way. But another shape loomed out of the darkness, blocking that way, too. Ugly had come round the other side. I was trapped between them.

The magician was calling something out from the stage. Ugly produced what looked like a folding comb and pressed a button on the side. It was a flick-knife. About twenty centimetres of steel sprang out of his fist, slanting towards me. Scarface began to move closer. Ten seats and he would be on to me.

I had a wall behind me and people in front. I had nowhere to go.

Mr Marvano had finished what he was saying. There was a long pause. Ugly was closing in from his side, too. The flick-knife flashed momentarily in one of the lights trained on the stage. I looked back the other way. Scarface carried no weapon but his fingers, long and skeletal, stretched out towards my throat.

"And now, please, I require a volunteer from the audience." Mr Marvano had tried it in Dutch and found no takers so now he tried English. Only three seats separated me from Scarface on one side and Ugly on the other.

My hand shot up. "I volunteer!" I shouted.

Every eye in the theatre turned to look at me. A spotlight swivelled round and everything went white as it hit me in the eyes. Scarface and Ugly froze where they were, just outside the beam. Somehow Ugly had managed to spirit away the knife. Ignoring them, I clambered over a seat, almost landing in the owner's lap. But a moment later I was away, moving towards the stage while the audience urged me on with another round of applause. For the time being, anyway, I was safe.

Mr Marvano had wheeled a big, multi-coloured box onto the stage. It was about the size of a washing-machine with a round hole in the top and about a dozen slots around the sides. I didn't much like the look of it but it was too late to back out now. Mr Marvano grabbed my hand and beamed at me through teeth that looked even older than him.

"And what's your name?" he asked, again in English.

"Nick."

"Nick. Thank you. And now, Nick, I am telling you the trick."

He wheeled the box towards me and opened it. It was empty inside. But now I saw that if I knelt down inside it and if he closed it, I would be neatly trapped with my head protruding from the round hole at the top. I didn't much care for the idea. For a moment I thought of making a break for it and trying to find a way out of the theatre. But I had lost sight of Scarface and Ugly. And while they were around I was safer here, on the stage, in the light.

"I am calling this the Mexican dagger box," Mr Marvano said. He repeated the words in Dutch. "Now I am asking you please to step inside." I hesitated, then stepped in. The audience watched in silence but I could barely see them behind the glare of the spotlights.

I knelt down. Mr Marvano closed the box shut and pressed four studs, locking it. I tried to move. But the box must have been smaller than I had thought. I was completely trapped, with the wooden sides pressing against my back, my shoulders and my arms. From the outside it must have looked like I was taking a Turkish bath. I wasn't too happy about being on the inside. What was it he had said about Mexican daggers...?

"The box is locked – here, here and here," the magician explained. "And now I will get the Mexican daggers." He waved a finger at me. "Don't go away!"

There was no chance of that. Painfully, I swivelled my head round and watched him as he ambled off the stage. The audience laughed and I realized I probably looked even more stupid than I felt. There was a rack of silver knives hanging in the wings, but no sign of any technicians or stage hands. Mr Marvano reached out to take the knives.

But then Ugly appeared, suddenly looming up behind him. He lashed out with a fist, catching Mr Marvano on the side of the jaw. The magician crumpled. Ugly half-caught him but then let him fall, at the same time dragging off his tailcoat. It was a neat trick, but I was the only person who had seen it. A moment later, Scarface stepped out from behind the curtain. Quickly, he put on Mr Marvano's jacket. Then, pushing the rack of Mexican daggers, he walked onto the stage. The audience stirred, puzzled. I smashed an elbow against the side of the box. My old wound from the wheatfield flared up again. The box didn't even creak.

"Good evening, ladies and gentlemen," Scarface said. He spoke in English, perhaps for my benefit. "I'm afraid Mr Marvano has been taken ill. So he asked me to finish the trick."

He snatched up one of the daggers. It was even more lethal than Ugly's switchblade, about twenty-five centimetres longer with a wide, curving blade. The handle was decorated with some sort of fake Aztec design. Maybe the dagger was fake, too. But from where I was sitting, it certainly looked real.

Slowly he advanced towards me. I had never felt more helpless. I couldn't move. I couldn't breathe. All I could do was watch. And Scarface was enjoying every second of it.

He smiled at me, a smile that was full of hatred.

"Wait a minute..." I began.

"The first knife, ladies and gentlemen," Scarface said.

He slammed it in. I shut my eyes and winced. Was I dead? Was I even wounded? I opened my eyes. Scarface looked as surprised as I did. The knife had certainly gone in the box one side. It had come out the other. But it didn't seem to have gone through me.

The audience was surprised, too. They seemed to have woken up now. Perhaps they could tell that this new magician had a quality that the last one had lacked. Complete insanity, for example. They broke into louder, more enthusiastic applause.

Scarface picked up two more knives. Snarling, he plunged them into the box. Both of them passed right through without even scratching me. The audience clapped again.

Snarling and muttering to himself in Dutch, Scarface picked up the rest of the knives. There were twelve in all. One after the other he stabbed them into the box, each time waiting for me to cry out and then exit into a better world. But none came close. I was untouchable.

By now I was doing a good impersonation of a pin-cushion. The audience was delighted. There were no more knives left and, for that matter, no slots in which to stick them. But Scarface hadn't finished. His hand went into his pocket and when it came out he was holding Ugly's switchblade. He pressed the button and the blade shot out.

The audience fell silent. He bent down over me. I could see the veins throbbing under his skin and one of his eyes had developed a twitch. "There are no more holes, Diamond," he hissed. "This one is for you."

"Thirteenth time lucky?" I asked.

He snarled. "You were a fool to meddle in our affairs."

"I was only doing it for the medals, Scarface," I said.

"Goodbye…"

He took careful aim. This time he wasn't going to bother with the box. His eyes were on my throat, right underneath my chin. Slowly, deliberately, he lifted the switchblade in his hand.

The audience waited. In the wings, Ugly leered at me over the unconscious body of Mr Marvano. The switchblade stopped, high above me.

I shut my eyes and waited. There was nothing else I could do.

THE WRONG MAN

The whole scene was frozen in the glare of the spotlights: Scarface, the knife, the waiting audience. Then everything happened at once.

The knife flashed down. There was a gun-shot. Scarface screamed and reeled back, clutching his hand. The knife hit the stage and stuck there, quivering, in the wood. Ugly twisted round, trying to see what was happening. Scarface bent over his cradled hand and groaned. Blood seeped out between his fingers and dripped onto his legs.

"Good shot, Ted."

"Thanks, Ed."

"Lower the curtain, Red."

The men from M16 had sprung out of nowhere. Now they swarmed over the stage while the audience – evidently in a good mood – gave them a cheerful round of applause. Ugly had put up a token resistance. One of the agents had given him a token punch on the nose and now he was out cold. Two more of them dragged Mr Marvano off while Ed and Ted grabbed hold of Scarface himself. His hand was bleeding very badly now. Ted's bullet had smashed right through it, and I can't say I was sorry.

Red lowered the curtain. Ted came over to me. He was wearing the same dark suit he'd had on at the London International the first time we'd met, and the same sunglasses. But now he took off the shades and looked me straight in the eyes.

"Are you OK, kid?" he asked.

"Yes," I said. I was fine – except that I still couldn't move.

Ted opened the box. "That was some trick," he said.

"They probably do it with mirrors," I agreed.

Then Tim came in between two more agents. Ned and Zed, perhaps.

"We found him outside," one of them said. "He was hiding in a dustbin."

"Rubbish!" Tim exclaimed.

"Yes. He was hiding in the rubbish."

Tim shook himself free and came over to me. "Are you OK?" he asked.

"I'm fine," I said. But it wasn't true. I'd been chased enough. I felt as if I hadn't stopped running for weeks. I turned to Ted. Or maybe it was Ed. "Please. I want to go home," I said.

*   *   *

"I'm very glad to see you," Mr Waverly said. "As soon as I got a report that you were in Amsterdam, I realized that you'd gone after Charon. So I sent my agents over to look after you. They spotted you just in time. Luckily for you…"

Tim and I had been flown over to London and now we were back more or less where we'd begun; at Number Seventeen, Kelly Street. Only this time there was no Bodega Birds. The headquarters of MI6 was just how it had been the first time, with Mr Waverly examining us with his hooded grey eyes over the polished leather surface of his desk. Ted and Ed stood guard by the door.

"You may have rescued us," I said. "But it was you who got us into this mess to start with."

Mr Waverly shrugged. "That was really your own fault," he said. "How were we to know that Charon would try to kill you?"

He sounded innocent but I knew better. Mr Waverly had somehow let Charon know that we were working for MI6. He had drugged us and dumped us. We were his sitting targets. And when he had sent his men across to Amsterdam, it hadn't been to rescue us. It had been to find Charon.

"I expect you have a lot of questions," Mr Waverly said.

"I've got one," Tim cut in. "What happened to the birds?"

"The birds?" It took the head of MI6 a moment to work out what he was talking about. "Oh – you mean Bodega Birds. That was just a front. We had to do that. You see, we couldn't allow you to get the police involved."

"Sure," I agreed. "They might have found out that it was you who paid Charon to kill Boris Kusenov."

That got him. For one second his eyes were unguarded and I saw the panic that was hiding behind those small, faded pupils. Behind him, Ted and Ed shifted uneasily. All three of them were like guilty schoolboys who had just been caught smoking behind the gym. "How did you find out?" Waverly asked.

I reached into my pocket and pulled out the cheque that I had found in Charon's drawer. "I found this," I said.

Mr Waverly hardly needed to look at it. He knew what it was. He coughed and ran a hand through his hair. "I have to congratulate you," he said. "You've been very resourceful."

"So why did you do it?" I demanded. "If you wanted to stop Charon, why did you pay him in the first place?"

Waverly sighed. I think he was actually relieved to get the confession off his chest. "It was an operation that went horribly wrong," he began.

"I'm sorry," Tim chimed in. "I didn't know you'd been ill."

"I haven't been ill, Mr Diamond!" Waverly paused. This was going to be more difficult than he'd thought. "We had to find Charon," he went on at last. "Too many people had died. Not just in England. America. France. Even Russia. It was always Charon. So we decided to mount an operation to bring him in. To unmask him. And we came up with an idea. The simplest way to find him was to become his client."

"How did you do that?" I asked.

"It was easy. He had a number of agents working for him. The man who knocked out the magician, for example. We got a message to them. They passed it to Charon."

"So you hired him to kill Kusenov."

"Yes. We chose Kusenov because we knew he had no intention of coming to England. He doesn't like England. In fact he never leaves Moscow. In other words, in order to kill him, Charon would have to go to Russia. And so of course, there was something he would need..."

"An aeroplane?" Tim suggested.

"A visa. You can't enter Russia without a visa. Don't you see? It was brilliant. All we had to do was monitor all the people applying for a visa to Russia and one of them would *have* to be Charon. And of course if anyone who applied for a visa had only nine fingers..."

"So you never really wanted Kusenov dead."

"Oh no. That was just the point. We were certain that Charon would be unable to kill him. He was meant to be an impossible target."

Suddenly I understood. Waverly was right. It had been a brilliant plan until it had gone terribly wrong. "But Kusenov decided to come to England after all!" I said.

"Exactly. That wretched painting, 'The Tsar's Feast', came up for auction at Sotheby's. Kusenov was a collector, and he had this fixation about the artist, Salvador Dali. He believed the painting had to hang in Russia – so he came over to bid for it. It was the last thing we'd expected."

"I get it..." I said.

"I don't," Tim muttered.

I turned to him. "If Charon had killed Kusenov on British soil and the Russians had then found out he'd been paid by MI6—"

"It's too horrible to contemplate." Waverly finished the sentence. He had sunk into his chair as if he were deflating.

"You still haven't found Charon," I said. "Kusenov still isn't safe."

"My dear boy." Mr Waverly recovered quickly. "The man with the scar! He *was* Charon."

"Scarface...?"

"Yes. He's in a prison cell now. It has to be him. He has only four fingers on his right hand."

I thought back to the theatre in Amsterdam. I couldn't believe what I was hearing. "Of course he's only got four fingers on his right hand!" I exclaimed. "Ted shot the other one off!"

That sent a ripple of alarm through the three agents. Quickly they conferred. Then Ted spoke. "It's true I shot him in the hand," he admitted. "But I didn't see him lose a finger."

"He must have lost it!" I insisted. "He certainly had all his fingers when we first met."

Ted shook his head smugly. "Relax, kid. Your Mr Scarface is Charon, all right."

"Has he admitted it?" I asked.

"No. But we'll crack him."

Personally, I doubted Ted could even crack a walnut without help from a friend but I didn't say that. I turned back to Mr Waverly. He was my only hope. "Mr Waverly," I said. "I know that Scarface is not Charon. Please believe me. You've got the wrong man."

But Mr Waverly wasn't having any of it. Suddenly he was all suit and old school tie. "I think I can be the best judge of this," he said.

"Why?"

"Because I'm the head of MI6 and you're

142

just a fourteen-year-old boy!"

Tim shrugged. "He has a point."

I started to speak, then bit my tongue. There was no point arguing with them. I'd be better off working it out on my own. "What about us?" I asked.

Mr Waverly smiled. "You can go," he said. "I've had a word with the police. That business with the bank. Everything's been explained. You're no longer wanted."

We weren't wanted. Not in any sense of the word.

Tim stood up. "So that's it," he said.

"That's it."

"Right." Tim thought for a moment. "I don't suppose you could lend us the bus fare home?"

We walked home. Every step of the way the same thought went through my mind. They've got the wrong man. They've got the wrong man. I knew Charon wasn't Scarface. He had been in the room at the Winter House with Ugly and a third man. It was the third man who was Charon.

I thought back to the desk, the drawer with the cigarettes, the mirror and … something else. I couldn't remember any more. I was tired. I needed to rest. But I couldn't – not yet. They'd got the wrong man.

Tim picked up a newspaper on the way

back. Someone had left it on a bench and now that the adventure was over he was keen to cut out any photographs of himself. But there wasn't even a mention of him. He was yesterday's news, already forgotten.

We climbed the stairs into the office and while Tim went through the paper again I put on the kettle and made us some tea. By the time I'd carried it into the office and sat down opposite Tim, my mind had begun to click into action. Carefully, I set out the pieces of the puzzle and tried to make sense of them.

Charon.

A white hammer.

A mirror in a drawer.

South by south east.

We still didn't know what McGuffin had been trying to tell us. Had he really wanted us to travel south on the South East rail network? Was that all it boiled down to? I still couldn't believe it could have been as unimportant as that. I thought back to the moment he had died, struggling to speak in Tim's arms, with the train thundering past overhead.

"They're auctioning that painting today," Tim said. He folded the paper in half and tapped one of the articles.

South by south east.

"There's a story about it here."

"A story about what?"

"The painting." He read out the headline.

144

"Sotheby's. 'Tsar's Feast'."

South by...

I sat up. "What?"

Tim sighed. "I was just telling you—"

"I know. What did you say? The headline..."

Tim waved the paper in my direction. "'The Tsar's Feast'! It's the first lot to come under the hammer this afternoon."

I snatched the paper. "Of course!" I shouted. "You've done it, Tim! You're brilliant!"

Tim smiled. "Yeah. Sure I am." The smile faded. "Why? What have I done?"

"You've just said it. The hammer...!"

"Where?"

"At Sotheby's!" I turned the paper round and showed him the headline. "That's what McGuffin was trying to tell you. But what with the train and everything you didn't hear him properly."

"What?"

"He didn't say south by south east. He said Sotheby's ... 'Tsar's Feast'."

I grabbed Tim's wrist and twisted it round so that I could look at his watch. It was half past one. "When does the auction start?" I yelled.

"Two o'clock."

"Half an hour. Maybe we can still get there in time..."

I was already moving for the stairs but Tim

stayed where he was, his eyes darting from the newspaper to me then back to the paper. "The auction?" he muttered. "Why do you want to go there?"

I stopped with my hand on the door. "Don't you see?" I said. "We've got to stop it."

"Stop the auction?"

"Stop Charon. He's planning to blow up Kusenov."

UNDER THE HAMMER

We managed to catch a bus outside the office – but were we going to make it? The traffic was heavy and the bus was slow. I looked at Tim's watch. It was already twenty to two. We weren't going to make it.

Tim must have read my thoughts. "Why don't we telephone them?" he said.

"They'd never believe me."

Tim shifted uncomfortably in his seat. I stared at him. "You don't believe me either!" I exclaimed.

"Well, it does seem a bit—"

"Listen." I knew I was right. I'd worked it out. I *had* to be right. "You remember the hammer we saw at the Winter House? An antique white hammer…?"

"Yes."

"It was an *auctioneer's* hammer. The painting is going under the hammer. That means, when it's sold, the auctioneer will hit down with the hammer."

"Yes!"

"Well, Charon's going to swap the real hammer with the one we saw. That must have been what they were talking about. The fake hammer will make some sort of electrical contact…"

Tim's eyes lit up. "You mean … Charon's going to electrocute the auctioneer?"

"No. It must be a bomb. The hammer will detonate it. That's how he plans to kill Kusenov. The moment the painting is sold, the whole place will be blown sky high!"

The bus slowed down again. This time it was another bus-stop and the oldest woman in the world was waiting to get on. Worse still, she had about fourteen shopping bags with her. It would take all day. Quarter to two. If the bus moved off at once and didn't stop again we might just make it. But the traffic was as thick as ever. I made a decision.

"We'll run," I said.

"What – all the way?" Tim cried.

But I was already moving. We had fifteen minutes, and a bus that was going nowhere. This was clearly not the time for a chat.

Sotheby's main auction house is in New Bond Street, right in the middle of Mayfair. If you ever find yourself in the area, don't try to go window-shopping. You won't even be able to afford the window. It's at number thirty-five, just one more smart door among all the others.

As we spun round the corner from Oxford Street and staggered down the last hundred metres, I could hear the chimes of clocks striking two. There was no security in sight on the door. Kusenov had to be there. The auction had begun. But Mr Waverly must have thought he was safe.

I reached the door, but even as my hand stretched out to push it open I was struck by a nasty thought. If there was a bomb – and I was pretty sure there was – it could go off at any time. The moment the auctioneer struck his hammer, that would be it. Did I really want to go inside? I glanced at Tim who must have had much the same thought. He was standing on the pavement, kicking with his heels as if they'd somehow got glued to the surface.

"We have to go in," I said.

"Nick…"

I left him out there. I'd made up my mind. I had to stop the auction. He could do as he pleased.

The auction house was busy that day. There were people moving up and down the stairs and along the corridor which must have led to a secondary auction room. Somebody pushed past carrying an antique doll, a label still attached to its leg.

Someone else went the other way with a bronze-framed mirror. For a moment I caught sight of my own reflection. I looked tired and bedraggled.

And young. Would they even allow a fourteen-year-old into the auction?

"Good afternoon, ladies and gentlemen…"

The voice crackled over an intercom system that had been installed above the reception desk. It was a plummy voice – the sort that belongs to someone who'd been born with a silver spoon in his mouth. Maybe Sotheby's were auctioning that, too. "Lot number one is by a painter who made an explosive impact on surrealism in Europe," it went on. "Salvador Dali. It is entitled 'The Tsar's Feast' and is painted in oils on canvas. I shall open the bidding at £100,000."

I turned to Tim who had decided to come in after all. He was standing next to me. "It's begun…" I said.

"Where?" he asked.

I looked around. "Upstairs."

But Mr Waverly hadn't completely relaxed his guard on Boris Kusenov. MI6 might not be involved any more, but he had handed the case over to the police and before we'd even reached the first step two uniformed officers had moved out of an alcove to block our way.

"Now where do you think you're going?" one of them asked.

"£200,000…" The first bid had been made. I heard it over the intercom.

I tried to push forward. "I want to go to the auction…" I explained.

"Bit young for that, aren't you?" The second policeman laughed. "Run along, sonny. It's adults only."

"You don't understand." I was speaking through gritted teeth. "You've got to let me pass…"

"£300,000 to the gentleman from Moscow."

"You heard what I said." The second policeman wasn't laughing any more. He was blinking at me with small, unintelligent eyes. I knew the sort. If he was reincarnated as an ape, it would be a step up.

"Please…" Tim muttered. "We want to see Mr Grooshamov."

"Boris Kusenov," I corrected him. "He's in danger."

"What danger?" the first policeman asked.

The intercom crackled into life. "£400,000 to the lady in the front row." Then immediately, "Back to the gentleman from Moscow. £500,000. Thank you, sir."

"You've got to get up there," I insisted. "Kusenov is in danger. We're all in danger. The whole place is going to go up."

"I think you'd better come with us," the first policeman said.

"£600,000 to the gentleman at the back."

"Go with you where?" I asked.

"Down to the station."

"£700,000 to Mr Kusenov."

"This is hopeless!" I wanted to tear my hair out. There were maybe only seconds left. And I'd had to come up against PC Plod and his best friend, Big Ears. There was only one thing left to do. It was the oldest trick in the book – but I just hoped they hadn't read the book. I pointed up. "Look!" I shouted.

The two policemen looked up. So did Tim.

I pushed my way through and on to the first stair. One of the policemen grabbed me. I broke free, then pushed him hard. He lost his balance and fell on to the second policeman. Tim was *still* looking up, wondering what I'd pointed out. But then both policemen collided with him and all three of them fell down in a tangle. The staircase was free. I bounded up.

"£750,000 to the young lady..."

The top of the stairs was blocked by two attendants who were coming down with an antique sofa. I skidded down onto my back and slithered underneath it. One of the attendants called out to me but I ignored him. I just hoped they would block the staircase enough to delay the two policemen below.

"£850,000 to Mr Kusenov. £900,000. Back to you, Mr Kusenov..."

I could hear the bidding but I couldn't see

the auction room. There was a large, square room hung with faded watercolours and prints but it was empty. Then I noticed an archway on the other side. I ran through, my feet pounding on the frayed carpets. At last I had arrived.

"£950,000 to Mr Kusenov. Do I have any advance on £950,000?"

I burst into the auction room and took everything in with one glance.

"Going once..."

There was the canvas itself, "The Tsar's Feast", that had started all the trouble by bringing Kusenov to England in the first place. It was bigger than I had imagined it, standing in a gold frame on an easel right at the front of a raised platform. An assistant stood next to it.

Then there was the auctioneer, a tall thin man in a three-piece suit. He was standing behind an ornate wooden desk. He was holding the white antique hammer in his hands.

There were about two hundred people in the gallery, all crammed together in narrow rows running across its width. Kusenov was sitting in the middle of them. He was everything I'd imagined he would be: grey hair, granite face, small, serious eyes, suit. That's the thing about the Russians. They always look so ... Russian.

Kusenov had been given a police guard –

and if I hadn't recognized him I'd have known him from the company he kept. Chief Inspector Snape was sitting on one side of him. A bored-looking Boyle was on the other. Why, I wondered, had they been chosen? The long arm of the law? Or the longer arm of coincidence? Either way it was bad news for me. Somehow I had to cross the full length of the auction hall – fifty or more metres – to get the hammer. I had two policemen who'd be arriving behind me any time now. And I had Snape and Boyle ahead.

"*Going twice…*"

The auctioneer lifted his hammer. I'd been standing there for only one second but already I'd run out of time. The hammer was about to come down on "The Tsar's Feast". There weren't any more bids. As far as this auction went there would never be any more bids.

Unless…

There was only one thing I could do. I lifted a hand. "One million pounds!" I called out.

The auctioneer had been about to strike down with the hammer. But now he stopped. There was an astonished murmur from the audience and everyone turned to look at me. I took a few steps into the gallery. The auctioneer stared at me. Then he turned to his assistant and whispered a few words.

"Who are you?" he demanded at last.

I could see he wasn't sure what to say. "I'm

a bidder," I said. "And I bid a million pounds."

All the time I was talking I was moving further into the gallery, getting closer to the hammer. I was aware of everybody watching me.

Out of the corner of my eye I saw Snape and Boyle stand up and start moving round to cut me off. But I had to keep going.

"You're just a boy!" the auctioneer exclaimed. The hammer turned in his hand.

"I know," I said. "But I get a lot of pocket-money."

There was another murmur from the audience. Kusenov was staring at me. Then Snape broke out of the end of his row and moved to the front of the room.

"Wait a minute," he called out. "I know that boy!"

"So do I," Boyle snarled, catching up with him.

The auctioneer gazed at the two men unhappily. "Who are you?" he quavered.

"We're the police," Snape snapped. "And the boy has got no money at all!"

The auctioneer looked as if he was about to burst into tears. Clearly he had never dealt with a situation like this. "Well ... please..." he stammered. "The last bid stands at £950,000."

"A million and a half!" I called out.

"What?" the auctioneer groaned.

"Boyle!" Snape shouted. "Arrest him!"

Boyle grimaced. "Right."

The auctioneer tried to ignore us all.

"£950,000," he announced. *"Going..."*

I took another step forward. "I'll buy the hammer!" I exclaimed.

"Going..." The auctioneer was determined to go through with it. I couldn't stop him.

Boyle was moving faster now, heading towards me. And then, at the last moment, Tim appeared in the archway at the back of the gallery. Somehow he had shaken off the two policemen.

"Where's the bomb?" he asked.

"Bomb?" Snape cried.

Everybody froze.

I lunged forward and grabbed the hammer from the auctioneer's hands. "Tim!" I shouted.

I turned round and threw it. The hammer flew high above the audience, twisting in the air. Tim reached up and caught it.

Boyle lurched towards me.

I stepped to one side.

Boyle missed and toppled forward. His outstretched hands went over my head and through the canvas of "The Tsar's Feast". There was a loud ripping sound as the rest of Boyle followed them, his head and shoulders disappearing through the frame.

In the audience, Kusenov fainted.

The auctioneer gazed sadly at the ruined painting. He shook his head.

"*Gone*," he muttered. What else could he say?

SPECIAL DELIVERY

"Do you know," I said, "there was enough dynamite under Kusenov's seat to blow up half of London.

"Which half?" Tim asked.

It was three days later and I was reading the newspaper reports of the attempted killing at Sotheby's. I'd been right about the hammer. The auctioneer's dais had been rigged up with a wire connected to a detonator and nineteen sticks of dynamite under the floor. If the hammer had come down, Kusenov would have been blown to pieces. It made me sweat just to think that I'd been there.

Of course, not everything had got into the press. My name, for example. According to the newspapers, it was Chief Inspector Snape of Scotland Yard who had raised the alarm and saved the life of the visitor from Moscow. I was merely an "unknown teenager" in the last paragraph who had disrupted the auction shortly before the bomb was discovered.

We'd heard nothing from Mr Waverly. I suppose he'd wanted to keep himself and MI6 well out of it. Since we'd saved his neck for him you'd have thought he might have dropped us a line or something, but that's the secret service for you. Happy enough to be secret. But not so keen on doing you a service.

And so at the end of it all we were more or less back to square one. It was five o'clock in the afternoon and a carton of milk sat on the table between us. I'm not sure if it was tea or supper. It would probably have to do for both.

"There were nineteen sticks of dynamite, Tim," I said, reading from the paper. "Charon really wanted Kusenov dead."

"Right," Tim said.

"It's a shame we never found out who he was."

Tim poured the milk. "He was a Russian diplomat, Nick."

"Not Kusenov. Charon. The police never found him."

"He was probably the last person you'd have expected, Nick." Tim raised his glass. "Mind you, I'd have worked it out in the end. I've got a sixth sense."

"Well," I muttered, "you missed out on the other five…"

There was a knock at the door. The last time

we'd had a knock on the door, it had cost us a week of our lives. We'd been chased, kidnapped, gassed, blown up, pushed off a train, shot at and generally manhandled and we hadn't actually earned a penny out of it. This time neither of us moved.

But a moment later the door opened and a motorbike messenger came in. He was dressed in black leather from head to foot, his face hidden by his visor. Almost subconsciously I found myself counting his fingers. They were all there. Five of them were holding a long, narrow cardboard box.

"Tim Diamond?" he asked.

"That's me," Tim said.

"Special delivery…"

The messenger put down the package. I signed for it and showed him out. By the time I had shut the door, Tim had opened the box and pulled out a single, red rose.

"Don't tell me," I said. "It's from Mr Waverly."

"No." Tim blushed. "It's from Charlotte."

"Charlotte?" The last time we had seen her had been at the station in Amsterdam. I had almost forgotten her. "What does she want?"

"She wants to see me." There was a white card enclosed with the box. "This evening."

"Where?"

Tim crumpled the card in his hand. "She wants to see me alone."

"How do you know?"

"She's written it. And she's underlined it. In red ink."

"You can still tell me where she wants to meet you."

Tim blushed and I realized he was still as much in love with Charlotte as he had ever been. It was incredible. I'd never once imagined Tim going out with a girl, mainly because it was impossible to imagine a girl who would want to go out with Tim. I mean, he wasn't bad-looking or anything like that. But if you were an attractive, sophisticated woman, would you want to spend your time with someone who still cried when he saw *The Railway Children*? Tim had no sex-appeal. He wore Dennis the Menace boxer shorts in bed.

And yet Charlotte Van Dam was after him. She had said so herself. And she'd underlined it. In red ink...

"It doesn't matter where we're meeting," Tim said. He had gone as red as the rose by now. What had she written on the card? "It's just me and her..." He went into the kitchen for a shower. I heard the rattle of the water hitting the curtain. Then there was the slapping of wet feet on floorboards as he went into his bedroom. He sneezed. The water must have been cold. There was the slam of a door. Then silence.

Twenty minutes later he reappeared in a

crumpled linen suit with a pale blue handkerchief in his top pocket. He had washed and combed his hair. He had shaving foam in one ear and a little talcum powder in the other.

"I'll be back later" he said.

"Have fun," I muttered.

"Don't wait up."

I finished the milk and threw the carton in the direction of the bin. It hit the edge and bounced onto the floor. What would I do if Tim moved in with a girlfriend? What if she was crazy enough to marry him? Maybe the two of them would go and live together in Holland – and where would that leave me?

I had nothing to do, so I started to clean up. I plumped up the cushions and rearranged the dust on the mantelpiece. There was a shirt lying on the carpet so I put it in the filing cabinet – under "S". That was when I found the gloves. They were on the floor, under the shirt. They belonged to Charlotte. She had left them behind when she'd run from Amsterdam station.

I picked them up, meaning to put them in the top drawer of the desk. But as I held them, they dangled down and I found myself staring at them. There was something wrong about them, something that didn't quite add up. I spread them out on the palm of my hand. It was obvious, but I couldn't see it. And thirty seconds must have passed before I finally did.

The left-hand glove had only four fingers.

It was as if someone had grabbed hold of my throat with a hand made of ice. I felt all my breath being sucked up into my chest. A little sound came out of my nose. Automatically, I scrunched the glove up in my hand as if I was trying to wring water out of it.

Charlotte's glove. Charon's glove.

And of course it had been obvious from the start. Only Charlotte had known that we were going to meet 86. We had given her the name of the ice-rink on the train. The moment she had arrived in Amsterdam, she had sent her two agents, Scarface and Ugly, to take care of the secret agent, to stop him from leading us to her. They must have arrived just after we did.

Her very names should have told me. Both of them began with the same four letters – Charon and Charlotte. So why hadn't I seen it? Maybe I was more of a sexist than I thought, but I'd never imagined an international killer being a woman. Everyone – McGuffin, Mr Waverly, Rushmore – had spoken of Charon as a man. Maybe that had been her most effective weapon. She had played on other people's preconceptions, hidden behind them. She had known. Nobody would ever suspect a woman.

But I should have guessed that, too. When I had searched Charon's desk at the Winter

163

House, I'd discovered a small mirror covered in some sort of powder. If I'd thought about it, I'd have known what it was: the mirror from a powder compact. With a sprinkling of face powder. It should have told me. It was a woman's desk, not a man's. And if I'd only seen that, everything else would have fallen into place.

I made a mental note to read more feminist literature – but not right now. Tim had gone to an appointment with a killer. If Charlotte blamed him for saving Kusenov … I had to find him before he reached her.

I ran into his bedroom. There were clothes everywhere – except in the wardrobe. He must have tried on everything before he'd chosen the linen suit. I started heaping up the trousers and shirts. I had to find the little white card that had come with the rose.

There was no sign of it. When I'd thrown out all the clothes, I started on his *Beano* collection, his bills, and six years' subscription to *True Detective*. There must have been nine layers between me and the carpet. If you wanted to hoover this room it would probably take you a week to find the Hoover. And I was looking for one small card. What if he had taken it with him?

What if …?

I forced myself to think. Tim hadn't gone straight into his bedroom. He'd taken a shower first. The shower…

The flat was so small, we didn't have room for a bathroom. The shower was at the back of the kitchen in a sort of alcove. I dashed in there, skidding on the floor which was covered in water. Tim's shower-cap was perched on the kettle. There were three bars of soap in the fridge.

But the card was nowhere to be seen.

I emptied every drawer in the place. Knives and forks clattered to the ground. Tea towels and tablecloths flew into the corners. I searched in the dustbins, the ovens, the cupboards … and finally I found it, pinned to the wall behind the door. It read:

Hampstead Heath funfair
7.00 p.m. Today
The Tunnel of Love
Charlotte

The Tunnel of Love! No wonder Tim had blushed so much when he read it. I looked at my watch. It was half past six. Hampstead was only a couple of kilometres up the road. I could still get there in time.

I was out of the office and running before I'd even started to think. Tim had an appointment with a killer. He was in love. I was going to save him. But I was unarmed.

As I hit the High Street and started up the hill, the night was drawing in. And somehow

I knew that the Tunnel of Love was going to be longer and darker than it had ever been before.

Whirling lights. Crowds. The smell of hot dogs and the jangle of different tunes fighting with each other in the warm evening air. The fair had come to Hampstead Heath and lay sprawled out across the grass for as far as I could see. It was five to seven. I had run all the way in the heat of the evening and for a moment I stood where I was, swaying on my feet. On one side of me came the wail of the ghost train; on the other, a rattle and a scream as a painted carriage whirred round a metal track. I can't say I'm a big fan of funfairs. I can't afford the fares so I never have much fun. But that evening the Hampstead Heath fair was looking its best. There must have been a thousand people there. Maybe more. Tim was one of them. I had five minutes to find him.

I pressed forward, past the coconut shies, the Hall of Mirrors, the helter-skelter and the big wheel. There was a blast of organ pipes and a huge merry-go-round started up, its multicoloured horses leaping and plunging at the end of their twisted golden poles. The Tunnel of Love was on the other side. I saw it and I saw Tim at the same time. He was sitting in a boat with Charlotte; number eleven.

166

Before I could reach them, the boat had drifted off into the mouth of the tunnel. A short, fat man pocketed the one pound fare and looked around for any other customers. But it must have been too hot for love. There was no one else around.

The Tunnel of Love was a big, wooden structure with plastic walls that were meant to look like stone but still looked like plastic. You went through it all in a little boat which was carried along on a shallow river. I almost smiled at that. Charon was the ferryman of the dead in Greek mythology. Well, it looked like Tim had just bought himself a ticket.

I couldn't go into the tunnel. I didn't have the money for a ticket and anyway I doubted if the man would let me ride alone. But if the entrance was blocked, the exit wasn't. I ran past the merry-go-round. For a moment the horses galloped beside my shoulder. Then I had left them behind me as I reached the end of the tunnel where the water gushed out before looping round to start all over again. Without stopping to think, I went into the tunnel.

There was only one way in and that was along the artificial river. The water lapped over my ankles as I splashed through the soft glow of this plastic lovers' world. If you've ever been into a Tunnel of Love, you'll know what I'm talking about. The river looped and zigzagged, going nowhere – slowly. There were a few plastic cupids – dressed-up shop dummies floating under the roof. I went past what must have been the high point of the ride, a couple of dummies done up as Romeo and Juliet.

The only sound in the place was the echo of the fairground music outside and the trickle of the water. Add a plastic skeleton or two and the place could have just as easily doubled as another ghost train.

A ferry bobbed round the corner and I stepped up onto one of the banks to let it sail past me. I watched it go with an unpleasant feeling in my stomach. It was number eleven. But it was empty.

"You ruined everything. You and your interfering brother…"

The voice was a malevolent hiss. I stepped forward softly. A thick black wire snaked in front of my foot. It was plugged into a second wire that trailed along to a socket in the wall. I realized that I had found the power source for the entire tunnel and at once half an idea came to mind. I leaned down and picked up the wire, cradling the connector in my two hands. Now, if I pulled the two wires apart, I would plunge the tunnel into darkness. The only trouble was, I'd probably electrocute myself at the same time.

"Charlotte…" Tim protested.

Still holding the wire, I tiptoed forward and looked round the next corner. Charlotte was standing on a triangular piece of dry land in front of a mock-up of Snow White and Prince Charming. But there was nothing very charming about her. She was holding a gun. And she was aiming it at Tim.

"I should have killed you when I had the chance," Charlotte rasped, and now I recognized the voice I had heard at the Winter House outside Amsterdam.

"But I thought you loved me!"

"Loved you? I can't stand you...!"

"Oh..." I had never seen Tim look sadder.

Charlotte raised her gun. "I'll enjoy killing you," she said. "And then I shall kill your brother. I enjoy killing people, you see. It's my business. But it's also my pleasure and so I'll build up an even bigger network of assassins. Everyone in the world wants someone else dead. I will provide the service. I will be the head of a multinational murder organization. I'll float shares on the stock market! I'll be number one."

She was insane. I could see it now. She was Charon. Pure murder.

Her finger tightened on the trigger.

I took another step forward – into sight.

"Tim!" I shouted. "Duck!"

I pulled the two wires apart.

There was a flash and the whole tunnel went

pitch black. But even in that second, Charon had wheeled round and fired; not at Tim but at me. I felt the bullet whip past my face. I fell back and dropped the wires.

"I'll kill you!" Charon screamed. Her voice was a thin, inhuman wail in the darkness. "I'll kill both of you."

I heard her step towards me. I couldn't see anything.

"No!" That was Tim.

"What...?" That was Charon.

There was a splash and – perhaps half a second later a terrible blue flash like nothing I had ever seen before. I was lying on my back, but in that flash I saw everything. Tim had realized Charon was coming for me.

He had pushed her into the river. But what he hadn't known was that the live cable I had dropped was also in the water. And when Charon had hit the surface, the circuit had been completed.

There was nothing we could do. There was another blue flash. Charon floated, rigid, in the water. Then the entire system short-circuited and the blackness returned.

We watched as the ambulance men carried Charon away. The electrical charge hadn't been strong enough to kill her, but it would be a while before she could stand up again and when she did the first thing she'd need would be a new hairdresser. The top of her head looked like a giant toilet-brush.

The police had been called and we were sipping cups of hot, sweet tea while we answered their inevitable questions. I suppose they thought we were in shock. But Charon was the one who'd got the biggest shock of all.

I didn't say very much. The fairground was still spinning and echoing all around us and I felt lost in all the noise and the bright lights. I had to face it: I had come to save Tim's life, but in the end it was he who had saved mine. I looked at him, sipping his tea from a plastic cup and suddenly I felt almost affectionate. Maybe I was in shock after all.

"Thanks, Tim," I said.

"It wasn't me who got the tea," Tim replied. "It was one of the policemen."

Behind me, the merry-go-round had started up again for the thousandth time, and that made me think. People got killed. Bad things happened. But at the end of the day, life was only another ride and, like it or not, I'd been given a ticket, so what else could I do but hang on and enjoy it and save the tears for when it was time to get off?

STORMBREAKER
Anthony Horowitz

Meet Alex Rider, the reluctant teenage spy.

When his guardian dies in suspicious circumstances, fourteen-year-old Alex Rider finds his world turned upside down.

Within days he's gone from schoolboy to superspy. Forcibly recruited into MI6, Alex has to take part in gruelling SAS training exercises. Then, armed with his own special set of secret gadgets, he's off on his first mission.

His destination is the depths of Cornwall, where Middle-Eastern multi-millionaire Herod Sayle is producing his state-of-the-art Stormbreaker computers. Sayle's offered to give one free to every school in the country – but MI6 think there's more to the gift than meets the eye.

Only Alex can find out the truth. But time is running out and Alex soon finds himself in mortal danger. It looks as if his first assignment may well be his last...

Explosive, thrilling, action-packed, *Stormbreaker* reveals Anthony Horowitz at his brilliant best.

"Suspenseful and exciting." *Books for Keeps*

"The perfect hero ... genuine 21st century stuff." *The Daily Telegraph*

POINT BLANC
Anthony Horowitz

Alex Rider, teenage superspy, is back!

Fourteen-year-old Alex Rider, reluctant MI6 spy, is back at school trying to adapt to his new double life … and to double homework.

But MI6 have other plans for him.

Investigations into the "accidental" deaths of two of the world's most powerful men have revealed just one link. Both had a son attending Point Blanc Academy – an exclusive school for rebellious rich kids, run by the sinister Dr Grief and set high on an isolated mountain peak in the French Alps.

Armed only with a false ID and a new collection of brilliantly disguised gadgets, Alex must infiltrate the academy as a pupil and establish the truth about what is really happening there. Can he alert the world to what he discovers before it is too late?

"Horowitz will grip you with suspense, daring and cheek – and that's just the first page! Prepare for action scenes as fast as a movie. A stormin' follow-up to *Stormbreaker*."
The Times